A BAXTER FAMILY
CHRISTMAS

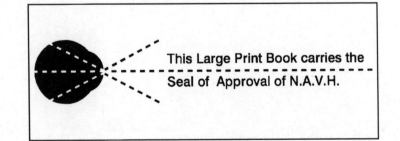

This Large Print Book carries the Seal of Approval of N.A.V.H.

A BAXTER FAMILY CHRISTMAS

KAREN KINGSBURY

WHEELER PUBLISHING
A part of Gale, Cengage Learning

GALE
CENGAGE Learning

Farmington Hills, Mich • San Francisco • New York • Waterville, Maine
Meriden, Conn • Mason, Ohio • Chicago

GALE
CENGAGE Learning·

LIBRARY OF CONGRESS CATALOGING-IN-PUBLICATION DATA

Names: Kingsbury, Karen, author.
Title: A Baxter family Christmas / by Karen Kingsbury.
Description: Large print edition. | Waterville, Maine : Wheeler Publishing, 2016. | Series: Wheeler Publishing large print hardcover
Identifiers: LCCN 2016042457 | ISBN 9781410496942 (hardcover) | ISBN 1410496945 (hardcover)
Subjects: LCSH: Christmas stories. | GSAFD: Christian fiction.
Classification: LCC PS3561.I4873 B39 2016b | DDC 813/.54—dc23
LC record available at https://lccn.loc.gov/2016042457

Published in 2016 by arrangement with Howard Books, an imprint of Simon & Schuster, Inc.

Printed in the United States of America
1 2 3 4 5 6 7 20 19 18 17 16

To Donald:

I remember the first time I wrote about the Baxter family. God gave me all the characters in a single cross-country flight, and you were there beside me . . . cheering me on. The Baxter family came to life while we were raising our kids. When they told stories around the family dinner table, we were doing the same. And when their kids auditioned for Christian theater, our kids were singing the same songs. Our family is — and always will be — inexorably linked with the Baxter family. So let me take this moment to thank you, my love. Thank you for creating a world where our love and life and family and faith were so beautiful I could do nothing but write about it. So that some far-off day when we're old and the voices of our children no longer fill the house, we can pull out books like this one and remember. Every single beautiful moment. I love you.

To Kyle:

You will always be the young man we prayed for, the one we believed God for when it came to our precious only daughter. You love Kelsey so well, Kyle. And you are such a great daddy to Hudson. Thank you for bringing us joy every day. We pray that all the world will one day be changed for the better because of your love and your life.

To Kelsey:

What an amazing season this has been, watching as a year ago — overnight — you became the best mommy ever. Hudson is such a happy baby, such a miracle boy. He is strong and kind and joyful, with a depth that tells all of us that some way, somehow, God is going to use him. And He will continue to use you also, Kelsey. You and Kyle and Hudson — and whatever other kids God might bring your way. Your family is a very bright light . . . and I know that one day all the world will look to you as an example of how to love well. Love you with all my heart, honey.

To Tyler:

Watching you take wing this past year has been another of life's great joys. Long ago when I imagined you graduating from college and moving out on your own, I thought it would be with tears and sadness. The quiet in the front room where once the sound of you playing the piano filled our nights. The empty space where you once made your bedroom. But this year caught me by surprise. I was simply too happy for you to find time to be sad. You are shining so brightly for Jesus — your songwriting, your singing, your screenwriting. God has great things ahead, and as always I am most thankful for this front-row seat. You are a very great blessing, Ty. Love you always.

To Sean:

I cannot believe what a year at YWAM has meant to your life. From the first day we held you, we knew your spirit was bright. You loved God and people with a passion and joy that defied your early past. Yet we agreed with you that it was time to take your faith to another level. You will never know just how thrilled your dad and I were each time you called from your YWAM mission trip, how we had tears in our eyes as you asked about each of the family and then offered to pray for us. Out loud. Over the phone. You left here a boy and came back a man, Sean. One we are so very proud of. I am convinced God has amazing plans ahead for you, Son. I love you forever.

To Josh:

This was a year of discovery for you, and for that I'm so grateful. You are walking into a future where being a spokesperson for Jesus can look a lot of different ways. He has gifted you with special skills that will cause you to be in demand in this world. People will always need your help, and along the way, I pray that you always give them more than they expect. Because people will always need a kind word, a gentle smile, a prayer and an invitation to church more than they will need any skills we can offer. I'm so glad you're my son, Josh. Love you so much!

To EJ:

What a tremendous time this is for you, EJ. You are doing so well at Liberty University, so excited about the career in filmmaking you have chosen. Isn't it something how God knew — even all those years ago when you first entered our family — that you would need to be with people who loved God and loved each other . . . but also people who loved the power of storytelling. I'm so excited about the future, and the ways God will use your gifts to intersect with the gifts of so many others in our family. Maybe we should start our own studio — making movies that will change the world for God. I love it! And I love you — always.

To Austin:

A very long time ago I scribbled out the years to come. 2001, 2002, 2003, etc. Under each year, I wrote the ages and grades our kids would be in — so I would get a quick glance at how fast the time would go. I remember writing out the number 2016. Because that was the year you — our youngest — would graduate from high school and move away to college. And now . . . here we are. I'm so grateful I can see you when I travel to Liberty University to teach. We will have many happy times together as you follow the path God has for you. Many breaks and special family times. But I miss you in the everydayness, Austin. You have been such a light in our home, our miracle boy.

Our overcomer. You are my youngest, and no question the hardest one to let go. The quiet here is so . . . quiet. Even with your dad's jokes and little Hudson's visits. So . . . while you're at Liberty, on quiet nights when you lie awake in your dorm, just know that we have cherished every moment of raising you. And we are still here. We always will be. Love you forever, Aus.

And to God Almighty,
the Author of Life,
who has — for now — blessed me with these.

THE BAXTER FAMILY: YESTERDAY AND TODAY

For some of you, this is your first time with the Baxter family. Yes, you could go back and read twenty-three books on these most-loved characters. But you don't have to read those, to read this one. In fact, there will be other Baxter books coming in the next few years. If you wish, you can begin right here.

At Christmastime.

Whether you've known the Baxters for years or are just meeting them now, here's a quick summary of the family, their kids, and their ages. Also, because these characters are fictional, I've taken some liberty with their ages. Let's just assume this is how old everyone is today.

Now, let me introduce you to — or remind you of — the Baxter family:

The Baxters began in Bloomington, Indiana, and most of the family still lives there today.

The Baxter house is on ten acres outside of town, with a winding creek that runs through the backyard. It has a wraparound porch and pretty view and the memories of a lifetime. The house was built by John and Elizabeth Baxter. They raised their children here. Today it is owned by one of their daughters — Ashley — and her husband, Landon Blake. It is still the place where the extended Baxter family gathers for special celebrations — like Christmas.

John Baxter: John is the patriarch of the Baxter family. He is a doctor, well known in Bloomington. He also teaches medicine at Indiana University. John's first wife, Elizabeth, died ten years ago from a recurrence of cancer. Years later, John remarried Elaine, and the two live in Bloomington.

Dayne Matthews, 41: Dayne is the oldest son of John and Elizabeth. Dayne was born out of wedlock and given up for adoption at birth. His adoptive parents died in a small plane crash when he was 18. Years later, Dayne became a very visible and popular movie star. At age 30, he hired an attorney to find his birth parents — John and Elizabeth Baxter. He had a moment with Elizabeth in the hospital before she died, and years later he connected with the rest of his biological family. Dayne is married to Katy,

39. The couple has three children: Sophie, 6; Egan, 4; and Blaise, 2. They are very much a part of the Baxter family, and they split time between Los Angeles and Bloomington.

Brooke Baxter West, 39: Brooke is a pediatrician in Bloomington, married to Peter West, 39, also a doctor. The couple has two daughters: Maddie, 18, and Hayley, 15. The family experienced a tragedy when Hayley suffered a drowning accident at age 3. She recovered miraculously, but still has disabilities caused by the incident.

Kari Baxter Taylor, 37: Kari is a designer, married to Ryan Taylor, 39, football coach at Clear Creek High School. Kari also runs the Bloomington Crisis Pregnancy Center with her sister Brooke. Kari and Ryan have three children: Jessie, 16; RJ, 9; and Annie, 6. Kari had a crush on Ryan when the two were in middle school. They dated through college, and then broke up over a misunderstanding. Kari married a man she met in college, Tim Jacobs, but some years into their marriage he had an affair. The infidelity resulted in his murder at the hands of a stalker. The tragedy devastated Kari, who was pregnant at the time with their first child (Jessie). Ryan came back into her life around the same time, and years later he and Kari married. They live in Bloomington.

Ashley Baxter Blake, 35: Ashley is the former black sheep of the Baxter family, married to Landon Blake, 35, who works for the Bloomington Fire Department. The couple has four children: Cole, 15; Amy, 10; Devin, 8; and Janessa, 4. As a young single mom, Ashley was jaded against God and her family when she reconnected with her firefighter friend Landon, who had secretly always loved her. Eventually Ashley and Landon married and Landon adopted Cole. Together, the couple had two children — Devin and Janessa. Between those children, they lost a baby girl, Sarah Marie, at birth to anencephaly. Amy, Ashley's niece, came to live with them a few years ago after Amy's parents, Erin Baxter Hogan and Sam Hogan, and Amy's three sisters, Clarissa, Chloe, and Heidi Jo, were killed in a horrific car accident. Amy was the only survivor. Ashley and Landon and their family live in Bloomington, in the old Baxter house, where Ashley and her siblings were raised. Ashley still paints and is successful in selling her work in local boutiques.

Luke Baxter, 33: Luke is a lawyer, married to Reagan Baxter, 33, a blogger. The couple has three children: Tommy, 13; Malin, 8; and Johnny, 4. Luke met Reagan in college. They experienced a major separation early on, after having Tommy out of wedlock. Eventually the two married, though they could not have more children. Malin and Johnny are both adopted.

In addition to the Baxters, this book will revisit the Flanigan family. The Flanigans have been friends with the Baxters for many years. So much so that I previously wrote five books about their oldest daughter — Bailey Flanigan. For the purpose of this book and those that might follow, here are the names and ages of the Flanigans:

Jim and Jenny Flanigan, both 45. Jim is a football coach for the Indianapolis Colts, and Jenny is a freelance writer who works from home. Bailey, 22, is married to Brandon Paul, 25. Bailey and Brandon were once actors in Hollywood — Brandon, very well known. Today they run the Christian Kids Theater in downtown Bloomington. Bailey's brothers are Connor, 19 — a student at Liberty University; Shawn and Justin — both 17 and juniors at Clear Creek High; BJ, 16, a sophomore; and Ricky, 13, an eighth grader.

CHAPTER ONE

Heavy snow clouds hung low over Bloomington, Indiana, the Saturday before Thanksgiving. But the atmosphere was warm and bright in the Clear Creek High School gym, where Ashley Baxter Blake sat next to her husband, Landon. On the floor with the ball was her fifteen-year-old son, Cole, whose freshman team was minutes from beating its crosstown rival.

The high-pitched sound of a whistle pierced the gymnasium. "Traveling!" The ref called Cole for the violation and instantly Ashley was on her feet. "Are you se—" She eased herself back down to the bleacher and bit the inside of her lip. Gradually she brought her hands together and clapped. "Here we go. You got this, Cole."

Four-year-old Janessa scrambled up onto Ashley's lap. "Cole's the best basketball boy in the world, right, Mommy?"

"Yes, baby." Ashley kissed her cheek. "And

the refs are just human." She met Landon's eyes over Janessa's head and managed a smile. She mouthed her next words to him. *I'm trying.*

Landon chuckled. "You've come a long way."

It was true. Cole was just a little guy when he first started playing basketball here. Part of the park league program. On his first game, Ashley had caught herself getting too enthusiastic, yelling a bit too loud. And yes, maybe a bit too concerned with questionable calls by the referees. Her attitude wasn't that surprising. Lately she'd been frustrated with her father and snapping at everyone.

Ashley drew a slow breath. She still cared about the calls and the scoreboard. But she'd learned a lot. Winning and losing meant nothing compared to the thrill of enjoying the game.

Cole played basketball because he loved it. Today. For now. If he scored twenty points and his team won, great. But the joy Ashley felt watching her son play had nothing to do with his points scored or an official's call or whether Cole played next season. Let alone whether he played college ball one day.

Even living here in the shadow of

Bloomington's Indiana University.

Amy, ten, and Devin, eight, sat on the other side of Landon. Devin tugged Landon's sleeve. "That wasn't traveling, right, Dad?"

Landon smiled. "If the ref says it's traveling . . ."

"Oh! I know!" Amy's eyes lit up. "If the ref says it's traveling, it's traveling!" She came up behind Landon and looped her arms around his neck. "Right?"

"Right." Landon grinned at Ashley and then he winked at Devin. "You have to play ten points above the refs. Just in case."

Thanksgiving was less than a week away, but Ashley Baxter Blake's mind was on Christmas, and the dinner her dad was trying to pull together. Which was the reason she felt so irritated.

By halftime Cole's team was up six points. The kids were hoping for the first snow of the season, so Landon agreed to take them outside to check. Ashley stood to follow but her phone rang. Her dad's name appeared on the screen. She motioned for Landon to go on without her. Then she took the call.

"Hey, Dad." She sat down again and tried to sound pleasant. "How are you?"

"Good. Beautiful day. It's already snowing here."

Ashley pictured it, the way fresh snow looked across Bloomington. The whole town would turn into a Norman Rockwell painting, the way it did every year at this time. "Amy and Devin will be thrilled."

"You kids always were when you were little!" Her dad laughed. "Of course, we always needed a big box by the front door for coats and mittens and boots. But that never stopped us!"

Ashley smiled at the memory. It seemed like yesterday when she and her siblings were the little ones, clamoring to get outside and play in the first snow. Now all of them were married with kids of their own.

Her dad paused for a moment, and Ashley could feel his tone change before he said a word. "Ashley, I think you know why I called . . ."

She closed her eyes. *I'm not ready for this, God. Help me. Please . . .*

"You and Landon." Her father sighed. "You haven't given me an answer about Christmas Eve. About dinner with Kendra Bryant and her husband."

Anxiety left an instant wake across the already troubled waters of Ashley's heart. She blinked a few times and stared at the small cross on the wall just above the side entrance to the gym. "I'm not trying to be difficult, Dad."

"I know." His tone was kind. "And I don't want to force your decision. It's just . . . I'd like a plan."

Thanksgiving was still days away, but her father had been talking about Christmas Eve since the beginning of November. Ashley and her siblings disagreed about how to handle their dad's request. But Ashley was easily the most concerned about the idea. "Landon and I talked. We don't think a family meeting with Kendra on Christmas Eve is a good idea. Maybe not ever."

Silence followed before her dad finally spoke. "I understand."

"You can still use our house. Landon and the kids and I will have dinner with his parents." Ashley tried to sound upbeat. But her effort didn't seem to be working. "I don't want to get in the way of your plans. But on Christmas Eve? I'm not sure how Amy would handle that."

"I like the idea of Christmas Eve. Because everyone will be together." Her dad sounded like he was struggling with the idea, also. At least a little. "I keep asking myself what would Erin want us to do?"

The mention of her sister made Ashley catch her breath. For a long moment she didn't speak. She closed her eyes again. *Erin should be here, God. We shouldn't even be having this conversation.*

"Ashley?"

"I'm sorry." She exhaled slowly. "What would I say to her?" What would any of them say? She spotted Landon and the kids entering the gym again, headed toward her. "Can I call you tonight? I'm at Cole's game. Halftime's almost over."

Her dad hesitated, but only slightly. "Sure." He paused. "Tell Cole I'm sorry I wasn't there. I had a few things to do around the house this morning. Next time, okay?"

"Of course." Ashley smiled. Her dad usually attended every game. Today, though, she was almost glad he wasn't here. She couldn't spend the hour talking about Christmas Eve and meeting the stranger with Erin's heart. It was all too sad.

Cole's team won the game and they drove home to play in the snow. Once the kids were outside, Ashley and Landon stood near the window. "I don't have peace about it. I don't think it's good for Amy to meet this Kendra woman."

"Honey." He turned to face her. "You're clearly uncomfortable with this." Landon hugged her and searched her eyes. "So we skip the Christmas Eve dinner this year.

We'll still see each other the next day."

Ashley looked long at her husband. She loved him so much. "Thank you. For understanding."

"Always." He shifted gears, grinned and motioned to the snow out front. "Let's go show the kids how to build a real snowman."

Ashley didn't call her father back until later that night when the kids were in bed. "Like I said earlier, Dad. Landon and I don't think it's a good idea."

"Okay." He was quicker to respond this time. "I understand. Really." He paused. "If you change your mind, just let me know."

His statement frustrated her. "Meaning . . . you hope we'll still join you?"

"Sure. Yes, that's what I'd like."

"But Dad . . ." Ashley paced across her bedroom floor. "I just got done telling you we won't be there." Nothing about this was easy.

"Just pray about it, okay? Can you do that for me?"

Ashley was near tears by the time she hung up. Her dad had never raised his voice, but he seemed unwilling to accept her decision.

After the call she found Landon in the kitchen washing the counters. "I talked to my dad."

He looked over his shoulder, his handsome face suddenly concerned. "He still wants us to be there?"

"Yes." Did she look as weary as she felt? She waited while he dried his hands and the two of them took seats opposite each other at the kitchen table.

Landon searched her face. "Tell me, Ash."

She nodded and her eyes found a spot on the table. "He wasn't angry or anything. But he wants us there." She looked up at him. "He asked us to pray about it."

"I'm sorry."

"Yeah." Tears filled Ashley's eyes. "I mean . . . of course we can pray. But think about how hard it would be."

"We don't have to be here." Landon covered her hand with his. "You can stick to your decision."

Ashley stood, paced to the sink, and turned again to face him. "Doesn't my dad get it? We're talking about Christmas!" She kept her voice low so she wouldn't wake the kids. But her tone was strained all the same. "Okay, so the woman has Erin's heart. She doesn't believe in God and she needs hope and direction. Her marriage is in trouble." Ashley walked from one side of the kitchen to the other. "I get all that. But why is that

24

our job? Couldn't we pray for her? Call a church in her area and try to get her connected?"

Landon shifted in his chair.

"I mean, there we'll all be. Standing around making small talk with this . . . this stranger. And the whole time she's only alive because Erin died. How are we supposed to have a beautiful Christmas Eve with all of that going on?"

"I hear you." Landon didn't look away, didn't argue with her. "Your dad means well. I believe that."

Ashley tossed her hands in the air and paced back to the sink. "That's the hardest part. Of course he means well. He always means well. He loves everybody."

A smile tugged at Landon's lips. "No matter how far gone they are."

The fight left Ashley and she felt her shoulders drop a bit. "Even me. Back in the day."

Landon gave a light shrug. "Just saying."

"Deep down you're not really on his side, though, right?" Tears blurred her eyes again. "Landon, really? On Christmas Eve?"

"I'm on your side, baby." He stood and came to her. "But I guess it's possible . . . Christmas Eve could change the woman."

A sigh slid from Ashley's heart through

25

her lips. "That's what my dad says." She came to him and wrapped her arms around his waist. "I just can't imagine it. Like what if I can't stop crying?" She pressed her head against his chest. "And what about Amy? How is she supposed to deal with that? Her mother's heart beating in the chest of a stranger? Right there in the middle of our Christmas celebration?"

"I get that." He eased back and looked into her eyes. "Maybe we should —" He seemed to notice something as he looked toward the doorway. "Amy. Honey, why are you out of bed?"

"You're talking loud." She wore a red flannel nightgown and rubbed her eyes, the light from the kitchen clearly too bright for her.

"Oh, honey." Ashley felt a rush of remorse. "I'm so sorry." She shared a quick glance with Landon. "Come on. I'll walk you back to your room. Me and Uncle Landon will be quieter. I promise."

Fifteen minutes later she returned to the kitchen. Landon was cleaning again, this time drying the stovetop. He set the towel down and turned to Ashley. "Think she heard us?"

"I asked her." Ashley put her face in her hands for a few seconds and then looked at

Landon again. "She said no."

"She must've heard some of it."

"I think so." Ashley took his hands. "I thought about talking to her, asking her about it, but even that could be devastating."

"True."

Ashley saw the compassion in Landon's eyes. He loved all their children so much. And he treated Amy like one of his own. Ashley kept her voice low. "She's had to live with so much loss."

"Just like you." Landon pulled her gently into his arms. "Like all of us."

She searched his eyes. "But you don't think anything good could come from meeting with the woman, do you? For Amy?" She paused. "We're the ones raising her. We should know what's best for her, don't you think?"

"I'm not sure." His words came slowly, his eyes shining with love for her. "Could there be some comfort in it? Knowing that her mother's heart saved the life of someone else?"

The idea hadn't really occurred to Ashley. She let her forehead lean against his. "I can't see that happening. It would be so sad."

"Well . . ." Landon eased back so he could

see her again. "We don't have to decide now. Christmas is still a month away."

Ashley nodded. She looked deep into his eyes, all the way to his beautiful heart. "Thank you. For listening to me."

"It's a lot." He brushed his thumb along her cheek. "Wanna pray?"

Her vision blurred with tears. She felt weary, afraid. "Yes. Please." She closed her eyes, but her fear and frustration only increased. The last few years had brought a gradual healing after the loss of Erin. Meeting Kendra would take her back to that terrible day in the emergency room, the day they found out about the accident.

Landon prayed out loud, asking God to give them wisdom and clarity about the possible meeting. He also asked that Ashley might have peace, whatever they decided, and that her father might think hard about the situation. When he was done praying, Landon ran his hands over her dark, shoulder-length hair. "Has anyone ever told you?" He grinned.

The heaviness in her soul lifted. She knew what was coming.

Landon raised his brow, his eyes sparkling. "You have the most beautiful hair."

She giggled. "Thank you, sir."

He moved in closer and kissed her. The

sort of kiss that still took her breath away. "Now . . . how about we get some sleep?" He kissed her again. "God will make the answers clear."

"Mmm." Ashley kissed him this time. "You're a good kisser."

"You, too." Landon took her by the hand and led her toward the stairs and their bedroom on the second floor.

Ashley would be thankful every day for Landon Blake. The man he'd always been. It was hard to believe she had almost walked away from him all those years ago. Back when she was angry at God and not sure of her place in her family.

As she climbed the stairs, Ashley remembered it all again.

She was the third daughter of John and Elizabeth Baxter. One of six kids, all grown up now. All married with kids. Her parents had seen her through those difficult years. When she'd come home from Paris alone and pregnant and rebellious.

But it was Landon Blake who had given his life for her and Cole. He loved Ashley's son like the boy was his own. Ashley's mother grew sick with cancer, but she lived long enough to see Ashley and Landon marry. They'd had three kids since then. One who only lived a few days before joining her grandmother in heaven.

Then came the car accident. Ashley's dear youngest sister, Erin, and her husband, Sam Hogan, and three of their daughters all killed that terrible day. Only their daughter Amy had lived. Raising her now was something else Landon took on as easily as he breathed.

That was the kind of man Landon was.

They reached their bedroom door. It was a miracle any of her family had made it through the heartache of that time. Erin's organs had gone to several recipients. And her heart had gone to Kendra Bryant. An atheist.

The woman her father had invited to join them for Christmas Eve dinner.

"Hey." Landon turned and put his arms around her neck. "You're thinking about it again."

She smiled. "How come you know me so well?"

"Because." He kissed her. "When you're sad . . . my heart hurts." He smiled. "It's always been that way."

"I love you." Ashley rested her head on his chest. She didn't know what she had done to deserve a man like Landon Blake. But she knew this much. No family could be expected to meet a woman whose heart once belonged to one of their own. Especially on Christmas Eve.

Not even the Baxter family.

Amy Hogan couldn't sleep. She lay in bed in her dark room and stared at the moon just outside her window. *You're here, God. I know it. Right beside me.* She waited a minute in case God wanted to say something. But Amy didn't hear any actual words.

Okay, God . . . so I heard everything they said. Now what am I supposed to do about it?

She rolled onto her side and tucked her hand under her pillow. Aunt Ashley didn't want to meet the woman. She thought it would be too sad.

But it was all Amy could think about.

What kind of a person was this stranger? What did she look like? Aunt Ashley said the woman was only alive because Amy's mommy died. *You must have really special plans for her, right, God? Because she got to live and my mommy didn't.*

Tears came. Amy couldn't stop them.

She didn't talk about her mom that much anymore. She loved Aunt Ashley and Uncle Landon. She felt like part of the family here. But every night before she fell asleep she did the same thing. She looked out the window, up toward heaven, and asked God to do something for her.

Tonight, though, she wasn't ready to do that yet.

Her thoughts were so loud she didn't want to sleep. What would it be like? Would the woman look like her mommy? Would she sound like her? Since she had her mommy's heart?

Amy wiped her tears with the sleeve of her nightgown.

Then a picture came to her mind of what it might be like.

It would be Christmas Eve and the woman would walk into the house. She would look like her mommy and sound like her. And Amy would run up and hug her and put her head against the woman and then . . . for the first time in such a long time, Amy would hear her mother's heartbeat. The way she used to hear it when her mommy would hug her and read to her and sing with her.

That would be really nice. Amy thought about that for a long time and her tears stopped. She rolled onto her back again and closed her eyes.

It's time, God. Like every night. Can you please tell my mommy and daddy and sisters that I love them. And I miss them. Amy waited. *One more thing, God. Please can you ask my mommy if I should meet this woman who has her heart? Okay. That's all. Thank you, God.*

With that, Amy yawned and a few minutes later she fell asleep.

But this time her dreams weren't about school or her cousins or her aunt and uncle. They were about a woman she had never met. A woman who looked and sounded like her mommy. And whose hug made Amy feel — if just for a little while — that her mommy was right here with her again.

CHAPTER TWO

Connor Flanigan loved attending Liberty University, but he had been looking forward to Thanksgiving break for a month. His sister, Bailey, had asked him to be a director for the Christian Kids Theater Christmas production.

He pulled into the parking lot in the heart of downtown Bloomington and looked at the clock on his dashboard. Five minutes early. He could hardly wait to start.

Three years had passed since Connor had been in a CKT play, but he'd never been part of the directing team. This time around the production was *A Charlie Brown Christmas,* and though it was a musical, the show was only an hour long. Which meant the rehearsal process would be quicker than for a full-length production. Auditions now and rehearsals in early December, when Connor came home for Christmas break.

The kids would perform just one show —

the Sunday before Christmas.

Easy enough, Connor thought. He would work with Bailey and her husband, Brandon, and a few others. Being away at school made him miss Bailey and Brandon. This time together would be the perfect Thanksgiving break.

Snow was falling, so Connor slipped into his heavy parka, shut the car door behind him and locked it. The air was so much colder here than in Lynchburg, Virginia, where Liberty was located. He buried his hands in his jeans pockets and walked across the street to the theater.

Auditions would be a blast. Growing up, he and Bailey were in a couple shows a year with CKT and they always looked forward to audition day. If things were the same as they were back then, the bond of camaraderie between the cast and crew and directing team would start today.

With the very first audition.

He spotted his sister as soon as he walked through the double doors. How crazy that they were this old now. Bailey, twenty-two, and married for two years. She and Brandon owned the theater and the retail space surrounding it. They had brought in tenants with a heart for missions and outreach. High-end tenants who had improved every retail space surrounding the theater. There was a thriving bookstore with leather chairs and a bakery and seating area at the back. A few doors down was a coffee shop where all the profits went to build wells for people in Africa.

Talk around town was that their work here had changed the very heart of Bloomington for the better. Owners of other commercial buildings had made improvements to their storefronts. They'd painted and added vintage brick and signage, and nearly all of them had planted trees and flowers that bloomed in the spring and summer. Downtown had a spirit of unity and kindness now that hadn't been here before.

Connor smiled as Bailey ran toward him. "Look at this place! It's beautiful."

"Thanks!" Bailey hugged him and stepped back. "It's only been a few months, but you look older." She grinned at him. "How's Liberty?"

"I love it."

"And your classes?" Her eyes were bright. "You're probably getting straight A's like high school."

"Not quite." He laughed. "But the classes are great. The professors really care."

She grinned. "I knew you'd do great there." She raised an eyebrow. "No girlfriend?"

"Not yet." He smiled. Bailey always asked about the girls in his life. They were still close like that. He linked arms with her and they headed for the judges' table, just in front of the stage where the kids would audition. "I switched from communications to film. Did I tell you?"

"No!" She stopped and faced him. "That's perfect. You'd be a great filmmaker!"

"I'd like to try. I've prayed a lot about it."

"Which reminds me, I talked to Andi Ellison the other day. She and Cody Coleman are back together. It's getting more serious."

Connor hesitated. He searched his sister's eyes. "Which is good, right?"

"Definitely." Bailey smiled. A long time ago she and Cody had been together. But they'd been friends first, and the friendship remained. The fact that Cody was once again dating Bailey's college roommate Andi was something Bailey seemed truly happy about. "Anyway, Andi's dad is still making Christian movies. When you get your degree, you'll have to talk to him."

"Definitely."

Connor was going to ask her how she and Brandon were doing when someone caught his eye. A girl just taking her seat at the judges' table. Connor hesitated and lowered his voice. "Who's that?"

Bailey turned and followed his gaze. "Her? That's Maddie West."

Connor stopped, his eyes still on the girl. She had beautiful blond hair and the body and mannerisms of a dancer. "Maddie West? Do we know her?" He glanced at Bailey for a moment and then back at the girl. "She looks familiar."

"I thought that, too." Bailey shook her head. "I don't think so. Her last name isn't familiar. And she never did CKT. She dances at the studio across town."

"I'm sure she does." Connor caught Bailey's raised brow. "What?"

"She's a senior in high school. She's my intern." She elbowed him lightly in the ribs. "A little young."

"Yeah." He grinned. "Maybe."

Bailey's phone buzzed and she checked it. "Brandon needs me backstage. Our pianist called in sick. We're scrambling to find someone else. Auditions start in an hour!" She headed toward a side door. "I'll meet you and Maddie at the table in a few minutes. I'll explain the audition process then."

Connor watched his sister go. Bailey clearly loved this, her world revolving around CKT. Her life here was so much better than the craziness of Hollywood and the constant insanity of the paparazzi. Everyone knew Bailey and Brandon and their love story. How Brandon Paul, one of Hollywood's top actors, stepped away from a life of fame to run CKT with his wife.

They'd been doing this for a few years now, and the business was thriving. Once in a while someone did a news feature on their new lives here in Bloomington. But for the most part Bailey and Brandon's days were beautifully normal.

They were doing what they loved.

Connor reached the long judges' table and took the spot in the middle, one seat away from the girl. She looked at him and smiled. "Hi."

"Hi." He returned the smile, his heartbeat doubled. "I'm Connor."

She faced him. Her eyes were the most brilliant blue. "I'm Maddie." She looked at the clipboard in front of her and then back at him. "I've never done anything like this."

"Yeah. Me, either." Connor laughed. "I used to be the one singing onstage. Did theater for years."

"Really?" She looked nervous at the idea. "I dance. But I'd be scared to death to sing. Especially up there."

"It isn't so bad." He leaned back in his

chair and took in the sight of her. She looked like an angel, her hair falling in waves around her face. *Focus,* he told himself. "So . . . how'd you wind up here?"

"I'm trying to get into Indiana University's teaching program." She wore black jeans and a black turtleneck. Cashmere, maybe. "This internship could make the difference."

If Connor hadn't known better, he would've assumed she'd spent most of her life starring on the stage. "How do you know Bailey?"

"I don't." The sound of a phone buzzing came from a nearby row of seats. "Sorry." She hurried for her cell and took the call. Whoever it was, she clearly wanted her privacy. She turned her back to Connor and slowly walked toward the far wall of the building. Probably her boyfriend. Connor tried not to stare. Where had he seen her before?

The call didn't last long. She breezed her way back to the table. "You were asking about Bailey. I mean, I know her because everyone knows about her and Brandon Paul."

"True." Connor grinned. "It's just . . . I feel like we've met before. Did you go to Clear Creek High?"

"My cousins did." She allowed a resigned laugh. "My parents weren't comfortable with a big public school. My sister and I attend Greenbriar Academy across town." A quiet beat filled the space between them. "Safe environment. Prep school. That sort of thing. A perfect choice for my overprotective parents."

Her overprotective parents? Connor wanted to ask what she meant, but Bailey was headed their way from somewhere behind the stage.

"We found a new pianist." His sister was happy but in a rush. "Doors open in ten minutes. Let's run down the role of a judge. Ready?"

Her instructions brought him back to reality. "Definitely. Very ready."

"Ready, too." Maddie flashed him a smile. "Though I have no idea what's coming."

"Okay, here's how it'll go." Bailey stood in front of the table as she explained the process. "The kids sign in at the back of the theater, where they each receive a number. Each child will have one minute to perform a song. The main thing is for us to be encouraging. This isn't *Fifteen Minutes.*"

Connor contained his grin. His sister looked like a kid again, her long brown hair gathered in a ponytail, flying behind her.

Just the way she used to look when the two of them spent year after year in this very theater, performing on this CKT stage.

Bailey was explaining the importance of writing notes during each child's song. "Your scoring sheets have categories. Was the song on key? Did the performer know the words? Did they make eye contact? Were they confident? That sort of thing." She folded her arms. She was breathless from talking so fast. "You'll score each singer on a scale of one to ten . . . ten being the best."

"And this blank section at the bottom of the sheet?" Maddie held up hers so Bailey could see it.

"Yes, good question." Bailey put her hands on her hips. "You can write anything in that spot. Try to be specific, so we can remember the performance later when we choose who will get a callback, and eventually who will get cast."

"Got it." Maddie stared at the sheet and then at Connor and finally at Bailey. "Do we say anything?"

"No. Don't worry about that." Bailey grabbed her clipboard from the judges' table. "That's my part. I'll call up each performer, help them with whatever they need through the audition, and thank them when they're done."

It was all coming back to Connor. Bailey made it sound easy. Audition day was always such a big deal when they were the performers. He remembered something else. "Tell her about the funny ones."

"True." Bailey smiled at Maddie. "A few of the kids are always funny. Some on purpose. Others because, well . . . this just isn't their thing." She shrugged. "Like I said, our job is to be encouraging. Keep it positive and lighthearted." She hesitated. "And try not to laugh."

"Perfect." Maddie leaned on her elbows. "Connor will keep me in line. He knows the ropes."

"Absolutely." Connor felt the chemistry between them. How had they grown up in the same town and missed each other all these years?

Bailey seemed to watch the two of them a moment longer this time. Then she buzzed toward the back doors of the theater. "Deep breath. Here they come."

As soon as the doors were open, more than a hundred kids burst into the auditorium and clamored for seats as close to the stage as possible. The energy was palpable, and again Connor remembered how it had been when he and Bailey were part of that group.

He leaned close to Maddie. "I still think you should've done CKT back in the day."

"Yeah, sure." Her eyes sparkled. "I would've been one of those kids everyone laughed at."

"Hey! We didn't laugh at anyone." Connor sat up straight again. "At least not on the outside."

Bailey had done this five times a year since she and Brandon took over the theater building. She easily organized the kids in groups of ten, and like that the auditions were under way. The first group sang fairly well. Connor noted that one of the boys would make a capable Charlie Brown. Two of them were at least good enough to sing in the ensemble.

After the tenth singer, Connor glanced at Maddie. "How's it going?"

"I'm keeping up." She winced. "Barely."

The next group wasn't as strong. Fourth up was a twelve-year-old kid in his soccer uniform. Probably trying to make it to an indoor practice after the audition.

"Okay, Garrett." Bailey nodded to the accompanist. "Go ahead."

If confidence were the only qualification, Garrett would easily win a lead part. He pushed his fingers through his blond hair and smiled. The music began and Garrett proceeded to sing "Ain't Life Fine" from *The Adventures of Tom Sawyer.*

His first crack came a few seconds in. The sound seemed to alarm him, but he kept singing. After that he cracked about every fifth note. At the judges' table, the three of them maintained pleasant smiles, nodding along, believing the boy could rebound.

He never did.

Connor wasn't even tempted to laugh. Poor kid. Every boy older than thirteen could relate to Garrett's situation. Last week the kid probably could've handled the song. This week? Not a chance.

At the break between groups, Maddie cast him a pained look. "That boy. I wanted to go up there and give him a hug."

"I know. Good for him for finishing." Connor checked his notes. "He won't get a callback, though. Out of kindness."

"See, that's what the directors would've said about me. 'Don't call her back. Out of *kindness*!' " She giggled as she locked eyes with him.

"Nah, never. Not you." Connor felt like they were the only two people in the auditorium. "You and I would've practiced together ahead of time so we'd both be cast as leads."

"Oh, really." Her eyes danced. Her voice

was flirty in a fun kind of way. "You and me?"

"Yes. Because we would've been best friends, Maddie." He grinned. "Of course. From the first moment we met."

"Of course." Her eyes made him forget the auditions altogether. "I guess we'll never know."

The auditions continued, and Connor was surprised to see more talented kids than he'd expected. After they'd listened to the last singer, Connor patted his sister's shoulder. "Gotta hand it to you, Bailey. You've built quite an army of performers here in Bloomington."

Bailey laughed. "The weekly classes have made a difference. Brandon's idea."

"Where is he?" Maddie looked sheepish for asking. "I mean, he works here, too, right?"

"He does." Bailey wasn't bothered. She was clearly used to questions about her husband. "He's in L.A. Producing a film on the apostle Paul. Brandon says it's going to be epic." She looked at her clipboard. "Let's figure out who we're calling back tomorrow."

For the next two hours they narrowed down the list until they had eighty kids they wanted to see the next day. When they were

46

finished, Bailey left to meet with her board of directors. Maddie had dinner plans with her family, and Connor had to get home to help his dad put together a new bookcase for the living room. Maddie was gathering her things, and again Connor couldn't keep from watching her.

"You're headed home, too?" She smiled at him. The connection from earlier was definitely still there.

"I am." He stood and grabbed his coat. "Walk you to your car?"

She gave him a shy smile. "I'd like that."

Outside the snow had stopped, but the ground was covered with a fresh six inches. "It's beautiful." Maddie lifted her face to the sky and breathed in. "I love winters in Indiana."

Connor laughed. "I prefer summers, but this is pretty. Definitely." He pulled his coat tighter around him. "So what do you want for Christmas, Maddie West?"

The snow was deep, so they walked slowly to her car. Connor was glad. He wished he had another hour with her, but at least he had this. She was quiet for a long moment. "This Christmas? Not the usual things." Her eyes found his. "Actually . . . I'm praying for a miracle."

He was touched by her honesty. "Really?"

"I know. It sounds cliché. Everyone wants a Christmas miracle." They reached her car, covered in snow like the others around it.

"Here. I can help." He used his bare hands to clear a part of the windshield.

"Were we expecting this much snow?" Maddie stepped in next to him and began brushing snow off the driver's door. As she did, their arms touched a few times.

"I don't think so." Connor made another swipe at the snow and as he did, a fistful sprayed Maddie's face.

"Hey!" She laughed and brushed it off her cheeks. She flicked some of it on him. "Be careful. I might not look like it, but I usually win every snowball fight!"

"Sorry." Connor chuckled. He eased his cold fingers over her hair, clearing away the snow still there. "I'll bet you do."

The moment felt breathless and intimate and fun. Like something from a movie. She turned to him then, the mood suddenly deeper. Her eyes were the most beautiful he'd ever seen. "About my Christmas wish. It's just . . . a lot's happened to me. To my family. I've asked for a miracle before, but it hasn't happened. This year . . . I guess I want to know God's still there. You know?"

Connor did know. His family had been through tough times and more than once he had reached a point where he had asked God for a sign. "I get it." His voice was quiet, their conversation muted by the stillness of the thick blanket of snow. "God doesn't mind when we ask Him to show Himself. To make Himself real."

"Yeah." The corners of her lips lifted a little. "That's it. Exactly." She looked off, as if the details filling her heart were too great to share. At least for now. "My sister . . . she has health struggles." Her eyes locked on Connor's again. "I guess I always feel like it's my fault."

"I doubt that." He wanted to hug her, but the timing was wrong. A few seconds passed, and Connor waited. He sensed there was more to this part of her story, but he didn't want to push. Maybe in time she would trust him enough to go into detail. For now he was grateful she'd opened up to him at all.

"Well, I need to go." She found her smile again. "Family dinner tonight." She dabbed once more at her pretty face. "Tomorrow's callbacks should be fun."

"Definitely." Now he hugged her, the sort of hug he'd give his sister. "Have fun with your family."

"Thanks." A shyness returned to her smile. "Nice meeting you, Connor."

49

"You, too. One of these days we'll have to have that snowball fight." He took a step back. "Oh . . ." He felt his smile fade a bit. "And I'll pray for your Christmas miracle. It'll happen, Maddie. I believe that."

Her smile warmed him to the core of his being. "Thanks. That means a lot."

Connor watched her start her car. With the deep snow, her tires spun for a few seconds before she got traction and drove away. Then he crossed the lot to his pickup. Never mind that winter was in full force and more snow was forecast in the coming days. As far as Connor was concerned it was blue skies and summertime.

All because of a girl named Maddie West.

CHAPTER THREE

Deep down, Kendra Bryant knew it wasn't just the busy time of year that kept her husband, Moe, at work making calls late that Monday night. Moe worked at an accounting firm in downtown Lexington, Kentucky, and year-end tax planning took up most of his hours. But lately Moe seemed to find whatever excuse possible to stay away from home.

Away from her.

She sighed as she grabbed a box of ornaments from the basement closet and carried them up the stairs and into the living room. Their first Christmas as a married couple — eight years ago — they'd worked side by side setting up the Christmas tree and hanging the ornaments. Kendra had made hot chocolate and they'd strung popcorn to hang on the branches.

Like something out of a Christmas card.

Kendra pictured life would always be like

that. Celebrating the holidays together, making time for traditions. Now she couldn't remember the last time Moe had helped her put up the artificial tree. He would come home late tonight and barely notice the decorations at all.

What's the point? She stopped and studied the bare tree. *Ornaments and twinkling lights don't make us a family.*

Kendra pulled out her phone and tapped her Pandora app. It was still three days before Thanksgiving, but Kendra liked putting the tree up early. She chose a Christmas station. The familiar beautiful sounds swelled through their small house, and Kendra turned the volume up.

Just enough to lighten her mood.

The first song was "Silent Night." Only instead of lightening the mood, the song gradually caused her to take a seat in the nearest chair. She and Moe were atheists. At least that's what they told people. But the truth was they both had doubts. Times when they wondered if they were wrong about God. Maybe He did exist. But neither of them ever pursued the possibility. With the way Christianity was viewed in today's culture, it was easier to simply not believe. Still, Kendra knew the words to "Silent Night." The way everyone did.

Silent night . . . holy night . . . all is calm . . . all is bright.

Was that true? Were things ever really calm and bright?

Kendra stared out the window at the Christmas lights on the house across the street. Everyone was getting into the spirit early. Everyone but Moe. *What's wrong with us?* The question wasn't directed at anyone but herself. Somehow it had to be her fault. She was the one whose health issues had consumed their marriage these last few years.

Kendra turned to the tree again. Something about the haunting melody took her back. Four years back . . . to the time when the virus first struck. Kendra had been completely healthy, a nurse at the local hospital. She and Moe were happy and talking about having children when one evening she spiked a fever. Highest fever Kendra had ever had.

It took her doctor a week to realize she had acute endocarditis. A raging infection in her heart. By then, the illness had done permanent damage. So much that she was given only a few years to live.

Even now Kendra couldn't believe she could go from being so well to so deathly sick in such a short time. After her doctor put her on the heart transplant list, Kendra struggled to comprehend what had happened.

Maybe it was her sickness, or the uncertainty of her future . . . but whatever the reason, her relationship with Moe became strained. He stopped calling her on his breaks and coming home for the occasional lunch. Her heart left her unable to work more than two days a week, and with the extra time on her hands, Kendra noticed more keenly the sad differences in her marriage.

Before she got the call about the available heart, Kendra was pretty sure things with Moe were over. They hadn't talked about getting a divorce. After all, Kendra was fading. Her doctor wasn't sure if she had six months to live, so splitting up wasn't a question. They were too consumed with her death to talk about anything else. But still they fought about money and how she could eat better to buy herself more time, how she wouldn't be sick if she had done a better job taking care of herself. Kendra actually figured death would be a welcome reprieve.

Then the call came.

A heart was available. It had belonged to a woman killed in a car accident. Kendra tried not to think about that part as Moe rushed her to the hospital. And two weeks later she left with a new heart.

The heart of Erin Baxter Hogan.

For a time after the transplant, Kendra and Moe got along better than ever. Life felt new and fresh and well again, and that spilled over into their free time. Moe even sent a letter to John Baxter, the father of Erin, to tell him how thankful they were for Erin's heart, and how her death had mattered.

Not long after, John Baxter called and connected with Kendra and Moe, saying he hoped they could all meet someday. He talked about Erin and the Baxter family and every other line was something about his family's faith or how he was sure his daughter was in heaven. That's when Moe became adamant about not meeting them. He wanted nothing to do with their faith. Plus, he thought getting together would be too much for everyone. Kendra disagreed. She thought there could be great meaning in getting to know Erin's family.

In recent weeks, whatever progress they'd made in their marriage had long since eroded. Kendra was alone much of the time.

The way she was alone tonight.

A different song filled the room now — "O Holy Night."

Kendra used a stepladder and wove a string of white lights through the branches of the tree. *O Holy Night . . . the stars are brightly shining. This is the night of our dear Savior's birth.*

The lights shone on their pretty tree tonight. But the birth of a Savior? Kendra pondered the possibility. Two thoughts had consumed her lately. First, the idea of meeting Erin's family and thanking them. She could picture looking into their eyes and letting them know that Erin's death was not in vain.

And second, the idea that there just might be a God, after all.

A God who came to earth as a baby that first Christmas morning.

The music kept Kendra company as she opened the box of ornaments. These were the antiques, the ornaments from her mother's tree. For a long time she studied them, staring at them and letting them take her back in time. Kendra never knew her father, and her mother had died in a skiing accident when Kendra was nineteen. Ten years ago. These ornaments, a box of photos, and a handwritten journal were all Kendra had left of the woman.

Slowly, with reverence, Kendra began hanging the ornaments on the tree. Her mother would want her to meet Erin's family. *Leave nothing unsaid.* That was her motto. And Kendra's mother had lived it out. Every bit of love and wisdom she'd had for Kendra was written in the pages of a journal Kendra had known nothing about. Until she found it in her mother's nightstand the week after her death.

Kendra had read it cover to cover several times since then. Apparently her mother had found faith in Jesus weeks before her death. Kendra and her mother had been planning to have coffee and talk about life that week — just after her skiing trip.

Instead Kendra had spent the week planning her mother's funeral.

"My mother believed in God at the end," she told Moe when they met. "She wanted us to believe, too."

But Moe only smiled the way he might smile at a silly child. "Believe in a God who took your mother away from you? What sense is there in that?"

Moe was alive and real and his argument made sense. That is, until recently.

The difference was John Baxter.

Kendra had been talking to the man on the phone lately. Every week or so. John was kind and intelligent and thoughtful. Whenever he and Kendra talked he always shared something about God. Including the last time, when John asked if Kendra and Moe would like to join the Baxter family for Christmas Eve dinner.

Moe was completely opposed to the idea. But the more Kendra thought about it, the more intrigued she became. Christmas Eve dinner would give her the chance to thank everyone in Erin's family. But even more it would let Kendra see the Baxter family's faith firsthand. Was it really possible? That an entire family really believed in God and His ways?

The song was wrapping up. *O night divine. O night. O night divine.*

Kendra hung the last ornament from the box of her mother's antiques. Every day the idea became more something Kendra wanted to do. And every day Moe found another reason why they should stay home. Mind their own business.

But who cared what Moe thought? He was constantly at work. The way he was tonight.

Kendra took a deep breath, picked up her cell phone, and dialed John Baxter's number. He answered on the third ring.

"Kendra. Hello!"

"Hi, John." She hesitated. Her new heart suddenly pounded in her chest. "I've been thinking about your offer. Christmas Eve dinner."

"Yes. I've been praying about that, too."

There he goes again. Praying about their possible dinner. Is that why I can't get the idea out of my mind? She squeezed her eyes shut. "I want to come. If you're still willing." Another pause. "It'll be just me. Moe . . . he's staying here."

"Okay." John didn't hesitate. "Please tell him he's welcome." John seemed to think for a moment. "You're okay with the drive here? By yourself?"

"It's three hours from Lexington. That's not a problem." Kendra opened her eyes and stared at her hands. Her fingers were trembling. "You're sure it's all right with your family?"

John's hesitation wasn't long. "Most of them. The others will come around."

She didn't like the sound of that. "But you'll tell me. If they decide it's better for me not to come?"

"I will." John paused. "What about Moe? Do you think he might change his mind and join you?"

Kendra appreciated this about John Baxter. In some ways John was like the father she never had. "He really doesn't want to. But maybe . . . if you pray about that, he'll change his mind." She glanced at her phone.

Moe should be home within the hour. "I'll keep asking. But either way . . . I want to be there."

The call ended a few minutes later. She would bring the trip up to Moe again. But she doubted any amount of prayer would make a difference. Kendra found another box of ornaments and worked until the tree was complete. She stood back and admired it. *Perfect, really.*

She sat down and studied the branches. She loved Christmastime. And this year — like last year — Kendra still worked only part-time at the hospital. More days to ponder life's biggest questions. Why was she here? Was it possible for love to last forever? And why did Erin Baxter Hogan die, but Kendra got to live? And of course, the biggest question of all: Were her mother and John Baxter right?

Long ago on a silent, holy night . . . did the story of Christmas actually happen?

CHAPTER FOUR

Maddie loved the day before Thanksgiving almost as much as Thanksgiving itself. Everyone who could help out went to Ashley and Landon's for what the Baxter family had come to call Pre-Thanksgiving.

It was midafternoon and in an hour everyone would be at the house except Dayne, Katy, and their kids. They wouldn't fly in from California until tomorrow.

"Maddie, can you help me?" Her fifteen-year-old sister, Hayley, was standing at the sink next to a bag of potatoes. She had a single potato in her hand and she was trying with everything in her to peel it.

But the move was too much for her.

"Of course. Hold on." Maddie had been polishing their grandmother's silver. She set down the fork she was working on and hurried to Hayley. She washed her hands and then gently took the peeler and the potato. "Here. Like this." Maddie easily shed the peeling into the sink.

"I can't make it do that." Her sister smiled at her, forever innocent in her approach to life. "You're smarter than me."

"No, Hayley." She slipped her arm around her sister's shoulders. "That's not true."

"It is." Hayley smiled again. "That's okay. I know it."

Maddie handed her the next potato and together they worked to peel it. The process was painstaking and awkward. But when they were finished, Hayley lit up. "I did it! You helped me, Maddie! Thank you!"

For the next several potatoes, Maddie stayed at her sister's side. By the time they'd completed eight of them, Hayley was brimming with confidence. "I really helped this year, right?"

"Definitely." Maddie smoothed her sister's blond hair off her face and kissed her cheek. "You're an amazing help, Hayley. No one cares more than you do."

Hayley giggled. "I believe you're right, Sister."

With that, Hayley yawned and stretched. "I'm going to go lay down. I want to help with the pies later on."

Maddie watched her make her way to the front room. She still went to therapy three times a week and these days, though she still moved slowly, she walked with barely a limp. Her studies were going well — as long as she had a tutor. But no matter how she improved, Hayley would never be exactly normal.

And here was the reason Maddie had asked God for a Christmas miracle. Not for herself, but for Hayley. A miracle that would prove to Maddie that God was there. That He cared about Hayley's future. That He hadn't given up on her little sister.

Because this was the secret she'd never told anyone. The fact that she alone was to blame for all of Hayley's struggles and special needs and handicaps. All of it was Maddie's fault.

And though she never talked about that, she felt it deeply. On the inside she had carried the reality of that every day for the last thirteen years. Each day at her lowest moments she could still hear her daddy's voice. "Maddie, keep an eye on your sister. Don't take your eyes off her. Don't let her go near the pool." She could hear her father's desperate cry as he looked for Hayley that afternoon at the birthday party. Still hear him shouting from the depths of his being. "No! Hayley, no!"

She could see him diving to the bottom of the deep end and swooping Hayley's limp body back to the surface.

Maddie felt her breath catch in her throat. She couldn't do this. Not here, the day before Thanksgiving. With practiced skill she stuffed her guilt and regret to the bottom of her heart.

"Maddie?" Her mother walked up, studying her. "You okay?"

A half a heartbeat and Maddie recovered. "I'm fine. Are Aunt Kari and Uncle Ryan coming today?" Their daughter Jessie was sixteen and one of Maddie's favorite cousins.

"I think so." Her mom kissed the top of her head and walked to her sister. "Hey, Ashley, have you heard from Kari?"

Maddie's Aunt Ashley was pulling her china down from a cabinet at the far end of the kitchen. "She'll be here any minute."

That was close. Maddie left the sink and returned to the silver. She picked up a spoon and rubbed it with polish. Her cousin Jessie usually helped her with this job. Once Jessie got here everything would be okay. Seeing Hayley struggle was always so hard. Maddie played tennis for the high school team and usually won every meet, while Hayley couldn't catch a tennis ball if her life depended on it. In the winter, Maddie would take to the ice rink and figure-skate with her friends. Hayley couldn't lace up a pair of skates. Even brushing her teeth was difficult for Hayley.

It wasn't fair, and all of it was because of Maddie.

But still she had never told anyone. Not even her mom and dad. As if by admitting her guilt to any of them, it might be too much. Too true. And then Maddie would suffocate from the shame and heartache.

Maddie's phone buzzed. She wiped her hands on a clean rag, and pulled her cell from her pocket. The text was from her cousin Jessie. *Hey girl, sorry I'm late. Annie wasn't feeling good, so my dad's staying home with her and RJ. We'll be there in a few minutes.*

A smile lifted Maddie's spirits. Jessie would help take her mind off Hayley. That's how it worked for her. The more distractions the better. Like the distraction of Connor Flanigan the other day.

After the callback audition, and after they worked with Bailey to choose a cast for the Christmas show, Connor had asked her out for coffee. At first the idea had made her dizzy in the very best way. The chemistry between them was incredible. But then Maddie reminded herself of Hayley. She could be friends with Connor. Nothing more. And so she had given herself permission to go — as friends.

Their time together came back to her, filling her mind and giving her a reprieve from her guilt over Hayley. They had taken a booth near the front window, and Connor had bought her a vanilla latte. Everything about the next few hours felt like a dream.

He was tall and handsome and funny. When he talked he seemed more honest than other boys their age. Like he had nothing to hide. And he listened to her. Really listened. That day she hadn't felt like any other senior girl at Greenbriar Academy. Connor Flanigan had made her feel like a princess.

One of the things she liked most about him was his love for Jesus. Connor had talked about God like He was a best friend. And something else. Connor wanted to be a prayer leader at Liberty next year. Maddie had loved it when Connor talked about that. He had also told her he wanted to work in film production after he graduated. "There's a lot of ways to be a light in this world," Connor had told her. "Making movies that help people see the truth about God — that's what I feel called to do."

She had told him about her parents being doctors and how their family ran a crisis pregnancy center in honor of her cousin who only lived a few hours and how after college she wanted to teach elementary school children.

Then he'd said something she would always remember. "I'm sure you'll be a great teacher, Maddie." He'd leaned closer, his eyes bright. "But if that doesn't work out, you can star in one of my movies. I couldn't find a prettier leading lady."

"Well . . . I'll have to keep that in mind." Maddie had grinned. She no longer felt her feet touching the floor. She had never liked any boy the way she liked him. "Just in case the teaching thing doesn't work out."

He'd told her about his family, too. How he had four brothers — three of them adopted from Haiti. And that his father was a football coach with the Indianapolis Colts.

"My aunt and uncle know a family with kids from Haiti. They came to a few of our family parties when I was younger." Maddie loved how he made her feel. Like she was the only person in the coffee shop.

"My parents probably know them." Connor grinned. "Seems like we meet more and more people who have kids from Haiti."

"Was it hard? Bringing in brothers from another country?" Maddie could only imagine the way Connor's family must've come together with the addition of the three boys. "Did they even speak English?"

"Not at first. We had a lot of funny moments in the beginning." Connor had laughed, as if he could see those days playing out again in his mind. "They were best friends, all three of them about six years old when they came home. They only knew Creole. It took about a week before my parents realized they needed to separate the boys at the dinner table. Otherwise they'd just talk to each other."

Maddie had listened, amazed. "I so admire your family. Y'all gave those boys a whole new life."

"In Haiti they used to eat dirt cakes just so they wouldn't be hungry. About six months after they came home, when they could speak English, they told us what their lives used to be like. It's a miracle they survived at all. God had a plan for them."

Now if only God had a plan for my sister, Hayley. Maddie had kept those thoughts to herself. They'd talked another half hour, but she didn't tell him the two things that might scare him off. The fact that she could never have a boyfriend. And the truth about Hayley, about why she had health issues.

She had wanted to hear more from Connor, but their coffees were gone and they both had places to be. "Someday you'll have to tell me about the funny moments, how things were in the beginning."

"I'd like that." Connor had walked her to her car again, and this time his hug had lasted a little longer. "I head back to Liberty on Sunday. After Thanksgiving." Their eyes had met and held. "I'd love to see you again before I go."

Panic had gripped Maddie. She hadn't meant to give Connor the wrong impression. *This coffee, it was wrong,* she'd told herself. She'd have to be more careful in the future. She had struggled with her response. "Uh, well . . . That weekend's pretty busy."

"Okay." Connor had looked confused. "Maybe we can just wait till then. In case you have time."

He'd asked for her number and again she had hesitated. Caught off guard, she had ultimately given it to him. But the truth was Maddie could never actually date him. She wouldn't let herself — that was a promise she'd made years ago. If Hayley couldn't do something, she couldn't either.

But even so her time with Connor had been breathtaking. She'd thought about him constantly ever since, replaying their time together, the way he looked at her. The way he made her feel.

He'd texted her at least once each day. Something that equally troubled and thrilled Maddie. No matter how much she liked Connor Flanigan, she would not date him. Not unless God opened that possibility for Hayley someday. Maddie hadn't dated or been to dances. She always found a reason. Too busy or not interested in high school events.

But the truth was something she didn't tell anyone. Not even her parents.

The fact that she alone had ruined Hayley's life. Her sister would be perfectly healthy if it wasn't for her.

Besides, if she was ever honest about what she'd done, how she was to blame for Hayley's accident, no guy would ever want her. Especially not someone as wonderful as Connor Flanigan.

Maddie was halfway through the silver when Jessie arrived. She hurried to Maddie and took hold of both her hands. "Tell me about this Connor! What's he like?"

"Shhh." Maddie looked around. "I don't want Cole to hear." She glanced at her other cousin, sharpening the carving knife across the kitchen. "He'll tell everyone."

"True." Jessie lowered her voice. "Cole means well. You know that."

"He does." Maddie kept her voice low. "But Connor and I are just friends. That's all it'll end up being, I'm sure. So no need to tell anyone."

"I get it." Jessie grabbed a spoon and began polishing. "Just friends?" Her look said she doubted the idea.

"Yes." Maddie allowed a smile. "But you should've seen him, Jess. He's so cute."

"Yeah. That's what I thought." She laughed.

Maddie loved how the Baxter cousins were all best friends. She was the oldest, and then Jessie, who was sixteen. Next came Cole and Hayley — both fifteen — and Tommy, who was two years younger. The older cousins loved being together and for the most part they knew everything about each other. Same with the younger group — but they were too little to do more than run around and play together.

Jessie dropped her voice even more. "So tell me about him."

"He's just a friend." Maddie smiled, careful to guard her heart. "But he's the greatest guy, Jess. He is so kind. And he's a freshman at Liberty University."

"Wow." Jessie's eyes lit up. "And he loves Jesus?"

"He does. And he's funny."

Just then, Hayley walked into the room again. She crossed the kitchen to the spot where Maddie and Jessie were working. "Can I help?"

"Yes, of course." Maddie found a soft rag and dipped it in the polish. "Just choose a fork or a spoon and rub the cloth over it till it shines."

"Like the top of the Chrysler Building!" Hayley grinned. She was always quoting lines from the musical *Annie*. It was her favorite show.

"Yes." Maddie gave her sister a side hug. No one loved Hayley more than she did. But the reminder of her sister's limitations stalled the conversation with Jessie. Hayley tried to polish a spoon, and for the most part she got the job done. But Maddie and Jessie each cleaned several in the same time.

That night, long after Maddie and Hayley and their parents had returned to their estate home in Clear Creek, Maddie thought about Connor and how she wasn't sure she could ever tell him the real story about Hayley. Her mom seemed to notice her quietness.

"You sure you're okay, honey?" Her mother had stopped by Maddie's room as she was getting ready to climb into bed.

"I'm fine." She remembered to smile.

72

"Mom, did you ever pray for a Christmas miracle?"

Her mom was pretty, long and lean with dark hair cut short to her face. She was more serious than Maddie, more left-brained. But she always made an effort to connect with Maddie and Hayley. When they needed clothes, she made a mother-daughter date out of the occasion. Once every few weeks she would take them both for coffee. Creating moments that mattered.

She turned off the bedroom light, walked to Maddie's bed and sat on the edge. "You mean specifically? Like that God would create something miraculous because it's Christmastime?"

Maddie thought for a minute. "Sort of. Like some miracle that . . . you know, proved He was real. You know?"

"Honey . . ." The beginning of alarm fell like a shadow over her mom's face. "You're doubting that God's real?"

"No. Nothing like that." Maddie's answer was quick. "I mean . . . not really." She hesitated and some of the thoughts troubling the water of her soul rose to the surface. "But think about it, Mom. Hayley? And Aunt Erin and Uncle Sam, their whole family? Only little Amy lives through the accident?" Tears welled in her eyes. "Wouldn't

73

it be nice to just know for sure that God is here . . . and He loves us?"

"Yes." Her mom exhaled and nodded. Slowly. "God's done that hundreds of times for us over the years."

"For you, maybe. But not for me. Like . . . I'm getting older and, I mean . . . it would just be nice."

"Mmm." Her mother brushed back a few strands of hair from Maddie's face. "Yes. I suppose it would be." She bent down and kissed Maddie's forehead. "I'll pray for that, too. Okay?"

"Thanks." A sense of peace and order settled over Maddie. "I figure it can't hurt to ask."

"True." Her mom glanced at Maddie's phone, charging on her bedside table. "Have you heard from the boy you met at the theater?"

"Earlier." She smiled. "He was busy with his family tonight. They live in Clear Creek. Near the golf course."

"Well . . . maybe you can invite him over."

The reality of the situation knocked some of the joy from her heart. "He's going back to college on Sunday."

"And back home again soon, right?"

"Yes." She hadn't thought about that. Connor would be home in time for the three weeks of rehearsals at CKT. Through most of December they'd be seeing each other every night at practice. "We'll see."

Her mom stood. "Well, goodnight, honey. Keep Jesus close." It was the same thing she said every night. To Maddie and to Hayley, who slept in the next room.

"As close as my heart. Love you."

"Love you, too." Her mom paused near the bedroom door. "Thanks for telling me about the boy. Connor, right?"

"Yes." Maddie felt butterflies in her stomach at the mention of his name.

"And about the Christmas miracle."

"You're welcome." Maddie smiled through the darkness of the room.

Her mom shut the door behind her, and for a long time Maddie stared out the window. On some nights — like this one — she could see the stars over Clear Creek. The way God had set them in the sky. "I know you're there, God," she whispered. "No one else could hang the stars in the sky."

She was quiet, waiting in case God wanted to say something back.

"Anyway. So I'm praying again for a Christmas miracle. Not really for me, but for Hayley. That she'll get a little better. Even between now and Christmas." Maddie waited again. "I know you love Hayley, God. And you love me and my parents. But if You could just give me a sign. Some proof that You're working things out. Thank You, God. Really."

After the prayer, Maddie rolled onto her back. Sometimes she wondered if she should trust her mom with her guilt over her sister. But then Maddie was afraid her mom would blame herself.

No, she couldn't tell her mom how she felt about Hayley. Better to keep her shame to herself. And as for Connor Flanigan, nothing would come from it. She wouldn't allow it. If Hayley could never be well enough to find love, then she would stay single, too. Anyway, eventually she would have to tell Connor about Hayley, and when she did, he wouldn't want to date her.

He wouldn't want anything to do with her.

CHAPTER FIVE

A clear blue sky and temperatures in the high sixties made John Baxter certain that this Thanksgiving Day would be one of the best ever. John and Elaine were the first to arrive at Ashley and Landon's house, just after noon. Elaine brought two pecan pies and John had a few containers of heavy cream — something he whipped up each year.

"Dad!" Ashley met him at the door. "Elaine! Happy Thanksgiving!"

Landon was right behind her, and from the kitchen came the voices of their kids — Cole, Amy, Devin, and Janessa. "Papa!" Amy ran up and wrapped her arms around John's waist. "It's going to be the best Thanksgiving ever!"

"I was just thinking that." John returned her embrace and hugged the others.

"They're my best pies ever." Elaine stooped down and hugged four-year-old

Janessa. "Is that a new headband?"

"It is." Janessa twirled. "Mommy's been teaching me how to walk like a lady."

John put his arm around Elaine's shoulders. "That's really something, sweetie. You're going to make a wonderful young lady. Just like Amy!"

They made their way into the kitchen, and as he set the cream down, John took a minute to appreciate the moment. Ashley had come so far in her faith and her ability to love well.

After her mother died, Ashley had expected her father would be single forever.

John had thought the same thing. His first wife, his first love, never should've lost her battle to cancer. But she had.

None of them had seen Elaine coming into the family, but when it happened, no one had struggled more than Ashley. But over the years that had changed and now there was no sign of tension. Not from any of his adult kids. All of them loved Elaine.

Same with the grandkids. Amy most of all.

And tonight, Amy was the one person John was concerned about — especially in light of the announcement he needed to make after dinner. Kendra Bryant was coming for Christmas Eve. The decision was final. He only hoped everyone would find a way to get on board. Ashley had adjusted to every other difficult situation in life. Amy, too. John believed they would both come to accept this as well.

Over the next half hour, the others arrived. Dayne and Katy, straight from the airport, and with them their three young children. The kids were tired from the flight, but in no time they pepped up.

"Wanna come see my dollhouse?" Janessa held her hand out to her little cousin Sophie and the two girls bounded up the stairs.

Dayne had the baby on his hip. "We've been looking forward to this all month." He shared a look with Katy. "And guess what?"

Everyone looked their way. "Another baby?" Cole was ready with a high five.

"No." Katy laughed as she linked arms with Dayne. "Not yet, anyway."

"We're staying here through the end of January!" Dayne looked beyond relieved. "We need more time at home. Less in Los Angeles." He high-fived Cole. "Which means we'll be over a lot more!"

"Great!" Cole nodded to the backyard. "I'll get things ready for the football game."

John smiled. He loved how his family enjoyed being together, how they got everything they could out of their holiday gatherings. The doorbell rang and this time it was Luke and Reagan and their family. By the time Elaine had set the little boys up with a bucket of building blocks, Kari and Ryan poured through the front door with their kids.

"The girls are upstairs playing with Janessa's dollhouse." Ashley pointed her sister's younger daughter toward the stairs.

And with that Annie ran after her cousins. The three girls were best friends, all of them blond, blue-eyed little princesses, with vivid imaginations and a love for singing and dancing. John was so thankful Dayne and Katy would be around more often. Sophie loved nothing more than to be here with her cousins.

Brooke and Peter arrived last with their girls. "I burned the first batch of peas." Brooke was carrying a large dish as she moved from the front door to the kitchen. "Had to start all over again! Sorry we're late."

"I told her to set a timer." Peter chuckled. "You know Brooke. She doesn't need any help."

"It's true." Brooke shrugged as she set the casserole down. "It's Thanksgiving! Can you believe it?"

The teenage cousins gathered in the front

room near the piano. A few of them had been taking lessons, and now that added to the fullness of the moment as Luke's Tommy played "Away in a Manger."

"That's beautiful, buddy!" Reagan raised her brow at Luke and John and then the others. "He's getting really good!"

"I remember when he got his head stuck between the spindles on your staircase." John grinned as the others laughed. "He's definitely grown up."

"Thankfully." Luke made his way around the room, hugging the others. When he reached John he stopped. "Dad . . . you always said you liked Thanksgiving Day almost as much as Christmas." He paused, his eyes shining. "I can see why now. There's nothing better than being together."

For a while everyone worked on the meal. Then at one o'clock — while the turkey was still cooking — they filed into the backyard for the Baxter family's annual Thanksgiving Day touch football game. This year Cole was in charge.

"Okay, if I read off your name, you're on Team A." He began listing names, including his — which he called last.

"A for Awesome!" RJ raised his fist in the air. "We've got this, team. Come on."

"Everyone else is on Team B." Cole looked

around. "Everyone get with your team. Then I'll go over the rules."

Tommy headed for the B team. "B for Best. It's our year, guys. Let's do this."

John and Elaine were on Team A, and as Cole went over the rules, the two of them shared a brief kiss. Elaine whispered near his ear, "Nothing like the Baxter family."

"My favorite people in all the world." John directed his attention to Cole. The rules were simple — much like real football, only tackling wasn't allowed.

The game got under way and after an hour of close competition, the A team won. Tommy shook his head in mock discouragement. "One more series and we coulda pulled it off." He pointed at Cole. "Next year, cousin!"

"We'll be ready for you." Cole laughed. "Unless we're on the same team."

Both boys laughed as the group headed back inside the house and washed up. Everyone found their places at the two long tables set up in the dining room. John's heart was full to overflowing as he watched his kids and grandkids take their seats. For a single moment, he let his eyes linger on the empty chair. The place they always set to remind them of those no longer in their midst. Their mother and grandmother —

Elizabeth Baxter. Erin and Sam and their three girls — Clarissa, Chloe, and Heidi Jo. And Ashley and Landon's baby, Sarah.

This year Ashley had set a separate table for the food. The turkey sat at the middle, where Landon was carving it. On either side were the mashed potatoes and the deep-dish sliced sweet potatoes. There was Cole's famous corn bread stuffing and the Baxter Christmas salad. Brooke's peas and Kari's cheesy biscuits. Reagan and Luke's home-made gravy, and Dayne and Katy's special cranberry sauce. And half a dozen other new salads and dishes that weren't part of their previous Thanksgiving spreads.

When they were all seated, Ashley turned to John. "Dad . . . would you say the bless-ing?"

This was their tradition, and each year John tried to customize the prayer to the circumstances. Some years had held great grief and tragedy. Others involved new life and hope. This year . . . well, this year they would find out after dinner about Kendra Bryant and her involvement in their Christ-mas Eve.

But not yet. John smiled at his family. "Let's pray." All around the table the Bax-ter kids and their spouses and children held hands, closed their eyes and bowed their heads.

"Lord, we come to You on this Thanksgiving Day with hearts overflowing with gratitude. Thank You, Father, that we can all be together today, here in Your presence. Thank You for our health and the way You are using us in our communities. This has been a year of great blessings, and for that we humbly thank You."

John paused, taking his time. "For all the ways You have blessed us and helped us in our schools and homes and places of employment, we are mindful that the greatest blessing of all is this — the joy of being together. The gift of each other. Thank You for today. Help us hold on to the precious moments it contains. Including this one. Thank You for our food, and for the hands that prepared it. We love You. In Jesus' name, amen."

Around him, from both tables, came a chorus of amens.

During dinner they went around the room and each person said what they were thankful for. John loved this part the most, hearing from even the youngest in the Baxter family, and getting glimpses of their hearts.

Not until dinner was over did John ask the older girls — Maddie and Jessie — to take the kids to the upstairs bonus room. When he saw the concern on their faces, John smiled. "Everything's okay. We just need to talk."

When all the kids were out of the room, John gathered his adult children and their spouses in the living room. "What a beautiful Thanksgiving." He smiled at them, thankful again for each one. As everyone settled in, John braced himself. "Most of you have an idea what this is about. Kendra Bryant — the woman who received Erin's heart."

Luke shifted in his seat. "You still want us to meet her . . . on Christmas Eve?"

"Yes." John felt the beginnings of tears at the corners of his eyes. "I invited her. And she has decided to join us."

There. The facts were on the table.

John surveyed the others, and the different ways they reacted. Katy and Dayne leaned into each other, their eyes still on John, still open to whatever came next. Ashley hung her head and so did Kari and Ryan. Brooke reached for Peter's hand and the two of them nodded. Like they were in favor of the plan.

John caught a quick breath. "I know not all of you agree with this. And it's true, we don't know this woman." Beside him, John felt Elaine press in closer.

"Isn't there a better time?" Luke sounded on edge. He sat up straighter, looking around the room. "Christmas is for family. This woman . . . she's a stranger."

"She is." John remained calm. He understood Luke's feelings. "The thing is, Kendra Bryant doesn't believe in God. She doesn't believe in Christmas." He looked around. "What better way for her to understand the truth than here? With all of us?"

Ashley rubbed the back of her neck and then lifted her eyes to John. "I can't do it, Dad. It would be too much for Amy."

"I understand." John nodded, his heart breaking. This was harder than he had expected. "I guess I keep asking myself . . . what would Erin want? And I know with every heartbeat that Erin would want to see Kendra Bryant come to know Jesus. She would want us to embrace her. Especially on Christmas Eve."

"I'll be here." Brooke sounded sympathetic, but certain. "To see firsthand at Christmastime the fact that Erin's heart saved the life of someone else? It'll be hard, but I want to be a part of that."

Peter agreed with her, and so did Dayne and Katy, Kari and Ryan. As they spoke up, Ashley sighed and stared at the floor. Landon put his arm around her.

Across the room, Luke released a frustrated sigh. "I can't do it, either." He looked at Kari and then Brooke and Dayne. "I'm not mad at any of you for agreeing to this. But I guess this year we'll have Christmas Eve in separate places."

"You can use our house." Ashley's slight smile didn't reach her eyes. "Landon and I will take the kids to his parents' house. It's only a four-hour drive."

John felt the weight of his decision squarely on his shoulders. "I'm sorry. I never wanted this to divide us."

"It won't." Luke nodded at his father. "It'll just be different this year."

The conversation stalled there. And even though no one exchanged sharp words or got angry, a tension remained. A tension that was rarely part of the Baxter family gatherings. The meeting came to an end, and the children joined them once more. Through dishes and dessert, nothing seemed the same.

For the rest of the night conversations between the adults seemed forced and unnaturally brief, no matter what John did to try to reclaim the mood. Within a few hours, everyone had gathered their children and headed home. The spirit of joy from earlier never quite resumed. John and Elaine were the last to leave. Ashley walked them to the door.

John hugged Ashley and then looked deep into her eyes. "I'm sorry, honey." He sighed. "I ruined everything."

"Honestly, you could've picked a better time."

Her comment stung. "I thought it might be the only time we'd all be together before Christmas."

Elaine looked uncomfortable. "I'll be in the car." She kissed Ashley's cheek. "Beautiful dinner. We'll talk soon."

"Okay." Ashley watched her go. When Elaine was in her car, Ashley shut the door and looked at her father again. "I mean, Dad . . . it's still hard enough celebrating the holidays without Erin and Sam and the girls. But to think about having that . . . that woman here for Christmas?" Tears welled in her eyes. "It opens up all the awful hurt all over again."

"I'm sorry." John couldn't find a way to make things right. "I guess we could've picked a better time to talk about it."

Ashley crossed her arms. "Or maybe only you should meet her. No one else wanted this." She wiped a tear from her cheek. "They're going along with it, but they didn't seek it out. Can you see that?"

John's heart sank to another level. He hadn't thought about that. "I don't know what to say."

A heaviness hung in the air between them. Finally Ashley took a slow, deep breath. "It's not your fault. You think it's the right thing to do." She wiped at her tears again. "It divides us, that's all. And I hate that."

John pulled her into his arms. "I hate that too, honey." He stepped back, his hands still on her shoulders. "Pray. That we'll get through this together. Somehow."

"We will." She nodded. Her eyes grew softer. "I love you, Dad."

"Love you, too."

John thought about his conversation with Ashley on the drive home with Elaine. It was true. They would get through this. But he hated seeing her so upset. Maybe he was wrong. Maybe he should've put the visit off until next year. John felt the sad heaviness straight through his soul. Either way, the decision had been made. He and the others were going to spend Christmas Eve with Kendra Bryant.

Whether Ashley and Luke and their families joined them or not.

CHAPTER SIX

All Thanksgiving Day, Connor thought his sister, Bailey, was acting strange. She and Brandon were more clingy, and several times Bailey was yawning when she should have been laughing.

"You okay?" Connor pulled her aside after dinner. "You seem tired."

A smile lit up Bailey's eyes. "I'm fine. It's just . . . yeah, I'm a little tired. No big deal."

Not until they were having dessert did the truth about Bailey's tiredness come out. She and Brandon kept looking at each other and grinning and finally Brandon held up his glass of cider. "Bailey and I have some news we'd like to share."

Connor watched his parents' attention turn immediately to Bailey and Brandon. The other boys didn't seem to catch on right away, but even they settled down long enough to listen.

"We found out earlier this week." Bailey

looked at Brandon and then back at their mom. "We're going to have a baby!"

"What!" Their mother was on her feet, rushing around the table to Bailey and Brandon. She threw her arms around the two of them. "Are you serious? This is the best news!"

Connor and their dad were on their feet at the same time, also hurrying over to congratulate Bailey and Brandon, and the other boys did the same thing. Against a chorus of congratulations and questions about the due date, Bailey and Brandon beamed with joy.

"All day we wanted to tell you." Bailey's smile filled her face. "But we didn't want to make dinner about us. So we decided to wait until now."

"The baby's due the middle of June." Brandon eased his arm around Bailey's shoulders. "She's been tired, but usually only sick in the morning."

The news was all they talked about for the rest of the night. Their mom shared how her pregnancies were all different, and Bailey talked about wanting a natural birth — as much as possible.

"That's wonderful." Their mother had moved next to Bailey at the table, and now she ran her hand over Bailey's back. "Just keep an open mind about the process. If you need medical help, God will show you."

As the conversation continued, Connor tried to grasp exactly what he was feeling. He was thrilled for his sister, obviously. A few months ago Bailey and Brandon had asked the family to pray. They'd been trying to have a baby for a year, so this was the greatest news. Definitely an answer.

But it was also a change.

For all their lives growing up, Bailey was his best friend. They did CKT together and stayed up late talking about life and relationships and God's plans for their futures. Connor thought Brandon was the best guy ever, the perfect husband for Bailey. But a baby would take Bailey one step further from the days when she had time for Connor.

He brushed away his feelings. No one was happier for Bailey than he was. But how many years before he would find his wife? Before he would once again have more in common with his sister and best friend?

Half an hour later, Bailey found him in the kitchen doing dishes. "Hey . . . can you believe it?"

"No." Connor grinned at her. "You still seem like you should be in high school."

"And not like that was five years ago

already." Bailey grabbed a dishtowel and started drying.

"Exactly." Connor shook his head. "I'm starting to feel like Mom and Dad. Always asking where the time goes."

They both smiled, the moment appropriately pensive. "What about Maddie?" Bailey raised one eyebrow. "The two of you seem like you're having a lot of fun."

"We are." Connor had thought about Maddie off and on throughout the day. "She's amazing. But there's something she's holding back. I can't figure it out."

"Maybe she's a little overwhelmed. You know . . . since you're a college guy and all."

Connor grinned. "I don't know. I guess there's no point really. After Christmas I'll be busy at school and she'll be here."

"I don't know about that." Bailey finished her work and hung the towel on the handle of the dishwasher. "If me and Brandon found a way with him living his crazy life in L.A. and me here . . . then anything's possible."

"Not everyone gets what you and Brandon have."

"Connor!" Bailey looked like she wasn't sure how to take his statement. "Tell me you're kidding. You're only nineteen years old. Whoever she is, she's out there. And when you find her, you won't have any doubts. Okay?"

"Okay." Connor smiled and gave his sister a quick hug. "You're right."

"I am." She looked straight into his eyes. "God's plans for you will be different than mine. But they'll be perfect for you."

Her talk encouraged him, and that night after Bailey and Brandon left, Connor went outside on the back deck and called Maddie. He shivered while her phone rang.

She answered just before the call went to voicemail. "Hello?"

"Maddie. It's me." Connor was suddenly not sure what to say. The cold air took his breath for a moment. "Happy Thanksgiving."

"Thanks." She sounded slightly uncomfortable. As if she was working at what to say next.

"Who'd you have dinner with? Just you and your parents and your sister?" Connor paced the length of the deck. Why did this feel so difficult?

"No. We went to my aunt's house. All my aunts and uncles and cousins were there. I think it was like twenty-seven of us."

"Wow." Connor thought about telling her Bailey's news, but he changed his mind.

Bailey might not want it public yet. "So you had a good time?"

"We did. How about you?" There was the sound of a girl's voice in the distance. She seemed to be talking loud.

"It was good." Connor stopped and stared at the snowy backyard. "Just the nine of us. But we had fun. Best turkey my mom ever made." He heard the voice again. "Do you have friends over?"

"No. That's my sister." Maddie must've moved to another spot in her house because the background sounds faded.

"Oh." Again the conversation felt stuck. Which was strange, because the first few days during auditions, he had felt a crazy chemistry between them. "So . . . tomorrow maybe we can have coffee again? Or are you doing the whole Black Friday thing?"

"We used to do that. Get up early. Hit the sales." She paused. "Not anymore. Anyway . . . I can't do coffee. I'm helping my mom decorate for Christmas."

"Got it. Okay." Connor raked his fingers through his hair and stared at the starless sky overhead. "Maddie . . . is everything okay?"

"It's fine. Sorry." She sighed. "I just . . . I need to get going. Thanks for the call."

"Okay." Connor told her goodbye and

hung up the phone. *Well, God . . . that's that. Maddie clearly isn't the girl for me.*

He slipped his phone into his pocket and headed inside to finish helping his brothers with the cleanup. But even though Maddie hadn't seemed interested, Connor couldn't stop thinking about her. When he went to bed that night, the last thought on his mind wasn't some happy memory of Thanksgiving or even his sister's wonderful news.

It was the face of Maddie West. A girl who had worked her way into his heart.

Whether he liked it or not.

Maddie lay on her bed, her face buried in her pillow. She had treated Connor terribly, and now all she wanted was to call him and tell him every reason why she'd been so unkind. It wasn't his fault. She simply had no room in her heart for a boy like Connor.

Better to end things now. Before they started.

She'd been fighting tears since she hung up the phone, and now she felt someone standing by her bedside. "Maddie?"

It was her mother. She rolled onto her side and looked up.

"Honey . . . what's wrong?" Her mom sat on the edge of her bed and touched the side of Maddie's face. "You've been crying?"

"I'm sorry. I'm trying not to." Maddie sat up and pulled one knee to her chest. "Today was the best Thanksgiving. Really."

"So what is it?" Her mom's eyes showed concern. "Are you missing Aunt Erin?"

"No. I mean, yes. Of course. It's just . . . Connor called me. He wanted to get coffee tomorrow but I told him no."

For a few seconds, Maddie's mother waited. As if she were trying to make sense of the situation. "All right . . . so . . . you meant to say yes?"

"No." Fresh tears filled Maddie's eyes. "I mean, yes. But I can't." She'd held on to this for long enough. Then she fell into her mom's arms and leaned her head on her mother's shoulder. "Can I tell you something? Just between us?"

"Of course." Her mom ran her hand along Maddie's hair and the back of her head. "I'm here, sweetheart. Whenever you need anything."

"Okay. We need privacy." Maddie reached for a tissue on her nightstand as her mom closed the door. "Hayley can never hear this."

"Okay." Her mother returned to the edge of the bed. "What's wrong?"

She sniffed a few times. "It's about Hayley. I never . . . wanted to talk about it. But I don't feel like I can move forward unless I do."

"About Hayley?"

"Yes." Maddie took a few breaths and looked into her mother's eyes. With everything in her she wanted to tell her mom the truth. How she had done something she had lived with every day since, and how because of that she believed Hayley's accident was her fault, and how she had lived with guilt and regret every day.

But she couldn't make the words come.

Instead she stuck with the same thing she'd talked about before. "I keep thinking about . . . how it's not fair that I get to live happy and normal and Hayley . . . she struggles. It's not right." Maddie wiped the new tears from the corners of her eyes. "Why can't God heal her?"

"Oh, honey." Her mom hugged her again. "He has healed her."

"Mom, she's not the same as other —"

"Maddie, don't you remember?" A new passion flared in her mother's eyes. "Hayley was never supposed to walk again. Never supposed to see or talk or ride a bike. Three months after the accident she could see me. Her doctor said it was a miracle, that there was no explanation for that. And a year later when she rode her bike . . ." Tears filled her eyes. "Hayley is walking proof of God's power. If she's different, it's for His glory. Because she should still be lying in a hospital bed."

"Mom." Chills ran down Maddie's arms and legs. "I didn't know that." She tried to picture Hayley wasting away in a bed, unable to see or talk or walk. This was something their family never talked about. Maddie narrowed her eyes. "Is that what they told you? When she was in the hospital?"

"Yes. They said she'd never get out of bed, Maddie. And so we begged God for a miracle. And God gave us just that. Beyond what we could've asked for or imagined. Your sister is healthier than we ever dreamed she'd be."

Maddie thought about that for a long moment. How Hayley was able to attend school and read and even polish silver. "They thought she'd never get out of bed?" Why hadn't she known this before? "I keep wishing God would help her. I didn't know . . . He already has."

"Well . . . now you know." Her mom smiled. "Let's pray."

Maddie nodded. This was something they hadn't done together in a long time. She and her mom held hands and prayed — that Maddie would feel God's peace, and that she would know the reality of Hayley's still-unfolding miracle.

When they finished, her mom stood. "I'm glad we talked."

"Me, too." Maddie remembered to smile. If only she felt better. "Love you, Mom."

"Love you more." She put her hand alongside Maddie's face and then she left.

The talk with her mother should've made Maddie feel less guilt about Hayley. But it didn't. That night as she fell asleep she thought about all God had done to heal her sister. How differently her life might have turned out if the doctors had been right. But she was still plagued by the reality — the fact that Hayley wouldn't have been injured at all if Maddie had only done her part. The details she hadn't shared. Because she still couldn't tell her mother the truth.

Let alone Connor Flanigan.

The thought of him made her smile. A dreamy kind of smile she'd never known before. It felt so good to be with him, to laugh with him. If she could, she'd hang out with him every day. But she couldn't.

Not now. Not ever.

Which meant that when Connor returned from Liberty for Christmas break, Maddie would have to do a better job of keeping her distance.

Because a lifetime would never be long enough to pay the price for what she'd done to Hayley.

Even if back then Maddie had only been a little girl.

CHAPTER SEVEN

An icy wind made its way through Bloomington the Sunday after Thanksgiving, but it didn't stop Ashley and Landon and their kids from making their way to Lander's Tree Farm just outside town. The place where most of the Baxters went each year to pick out Christmas trees for their respective homes.

Ashley and Landon led their family to the lobby first, where Kari and Ryan and their children were already holding two tables. Kari stood and hugged Ashley. "It's freezing out there."

"I told her to stay in here." Cole nodded to his uncle Ryan. "The men can get the trees this year." He grinned. "After hot chocolate, that is."

Ashley kept her scarf and gloves in place. "Might be a good idea."

Ryan and Landon and Cole left the table and got in line. Hot chocolate and home-baked cookies were part of the tradition. Ashley took the seat next to Kari, as Amy and Devin and Janessa squeezed in between Kari's kids.

"Have you heard from Luke?" Kari kept her voice low. "I don't think he's coming today."

"It's a hike." Ashley didn't want to believe their brother's absence was because of the Christmas Eve decision. "Twice here from Indianapolis in one weekend."

"They did it last year." Kari frowned. "I just hate the tension. Especially from him."

"I know." Ashley caught Amy watching from across the table. She dropped her voice a level. "Let's talk about it later."

Their father and Elaine entered the lobby. Like the others, they were bundled in winter gear. John unwrapped his scarf from his face as he approached them. "More snow in the forecast. Could be the coldest winter in a long time."

"Perfect for getting a Christmas tree." RJ grinned at his cousin Devin. "Plus we're mountain men. We're used to the cold."

"Exactly." Devin was a year younger than RJ, but both of them were in third grade at Clear Creek Elementary School. "I like Cole's idea. Girls stay inside and keep warm. Us boys can do the work."

103

"But what if we want to help pick out the tree?" Amy giggled at the boys. "Every mountain man needs a mountain woman."

Brooke and Peter and their girls arrived and after everyone had hot chocolate and cookies, they set out together to find their trees. The wind had died down so no one stayed behind. As the group set out, Ashley and Landon trailed along behind the others.

"Doesn't he get it?" Ashley felt her frustration rise to the surface again. "He didn't even ask about Luke. Which just isn't normal."

Landon eased his arm around her waist as they walked. "He's just enjoying the day, Ash. The rest of us are here."

"I know, but . . ." She walked in silence for a few moments. "He should at least be sorry. This was all his doing."

Landon was quiet for a long moment as they walked through the snow. Finally he moved his arm up around her shoulders and gently pulled her closer. "All I know is that your dad loves you." He kissed the side of her head. "Still . . . I'm sorry you're hurting. Really."

Ashley chided herself. "I'm sorry, too." She sighed. "This is a special day. I don't mean to be a downer."

104

Amy and Janessa turned back and ran toward them. "We're pretending we're lost in the wilderness." Janessa's eyes were bright with joy. "Okay? You two pretend with us." She waved her arm in a big circle. "Pretend it's a big storm coming and we have to hunt for our food."

Ashley stifled a laugh. "Okay! We'll protect you."

"And I'll do the hunting." Landon raised his hand. "You girls can help Mom find shelter."

"Yeah!" Amy clapped her hands. "Come on, Janessa!" They ran back to the front of the group.

Ashley laughed again. "How can I be upset about Christmas Eve when today is so good?"

"Exactly."

Ashley breathed deep, the fresh air cold in her lungs. "We'll deal with my dad's decision later."

They walked up a hill to a grove of pretty Christmas trees. Cole declared the area the best in the entire tree farm. Janessa and Amy and their cousins found a place they could all live if they never made it back to civilization. Ashley loved their imagination almost as much as Christmas itself.

In the next half hour each family found a

tree and the kids took turns using the saws. On the way back down the hill to the farmhouse, Ashley and her dad allowed some distance between them and the others. Despite the beautiful afternoon, Ashley felt her anger return. "You know why Luke isn't here, right?"

Her dad seemed caught off guard by her tone. "He said they had things to do."

"That's not why." Ashley worked to control her tone. "Dad, he's upset. I am, too."

"About Kendra." His words were more of a statement than a question.

"Yes." She forced herself to take a breath. "Christmas is a special time. Please . . . can't you reschedule her? Sometime next year?"

"Well . . . at this point, she's already confirmed." Her father looked at the snow-packed ground ahead. "Meeting her on Christmas Eve matters to me."

Ashley could tell from her father's tone that the subject was closed. "Christmas matters to us, too."

"I'm sorry you're upset, Ashley." Her dad narrowed his eyes. For the first time since the subject came up he seemed less sympathetic. "I thought you'd understand."

"I don't have a choice." She hated this, hated fighting with him. "You're not going to change your mind. That's fine." She steeled herself to the cold breeze. "We won't be there."

"You're worried about Amy." He gave her a sad smile, his woolen beanie pulled down over his brow. "I get that. But have you asked her?"

"Really, Dad?" She raised her voice, and then immediately felt embarrassed. The discussion was going nowhere. The wind had picked up again and with it came a wave of snow flurries. She moved closer to her father so he could hear her. "You want me to ask a ten-year-old little girl if she'd like to meet the stranger who has her mother's heart?"

"I don't know." Her father stuffed his hands deep in his pockets. "When I pray about it, I feel like somehow the meeting could be good for Amy. Healing, even."

"I don't think so." Ashley was beyond frustrated. "How about we agree to disagree. I just thought you could wait until after Christmas. Or until Amy's older. But it is what it is." She hesitated. "You have it your way and we'll have it ours."

He was quiet for a moment. The two of them still trailed the rest of the group — all of whom seemed excited over the trees the men were hauling back. "I'm sorry, Ashley. Really."

"Dad, if you were sorry you'd change this." She stopped walking as tears blurred her vision. "Don't you see that?"

"I can't change it. Not now." Her dad stopped and faced her. "I gave the woman my word."

"Okay." Ashley crossed her arms and started walking again. "Enough. Let's just drop it."

"Don't be mad, Ash." He walked beside her, but he sounded more upset than before.

"I'm not mad. Just hurt."

"I'm sorry." John shoved his hands in the pockets of his jacket. "Really."

Two hours later the trees were tied to their cars and after another round of hot chocolate, everyone left. Ashley realized after they were halfway home that she hadn't hugged her father goodbye. Which she hated. The tension between them was terrible. She and her dad were never like this. Ashley sighed.

Not until after Ashley and Landon and the kids were gathered in the family room setting up their tree in the stand did Landon look around. "Where's Amy?"

"Upstairs." Cole was lying on the floor, sliding the trunk of the tree one way and then the other, looking for the perfect spot.

"She was tired. Or cold. Maybe both." He shifted the tree again. "Hey, Dad . . . what about this?"

Suddenly Ashley had a terrible thought. What if Amy had heard the conversation between Ashley and her father? She was young, but she was keenly aware of discussions around her.

Especially where her mother was concerned.

Ashley padded upstairs and walked to the end of the hall, to Amy's room. The room that once, a long time ago, was Ashley's own. The lights were off. Ashley peered inside and walked softly to the bed. Cole was right. Amy was asleep.

For a long time, Ashley stared at the girl. *Lord, protect her heart. She's been through so much loss already. Please help us know how to love her. Especially now . . . at Christmastime.*

She bent down, kissed Amy's cheek, and left her to sleep.

They would talk about whatever Amy had heard, later.

Ashley and Landon brought out the boxes of ornaments and led the kids in a mass decorating effort. The two of them had to agree with the kids. This was the best tree they'd ever had. It was so pretty it didn't look real.

After a while, Amy joined them and she seemed as happy as the other kids. Excited about Christmas and thrilled to hang decorations. If she was upset about something said earlier, she didn't seem like it. Ashley decided not to ask her niece about what she'd heard. The question would just make the child unsettled. Best to leave the possibility alone for now.

Whether it was the cold air or the hike through the tree farm, after decorating the kids were more tired than usual. By eight o'clock they were all in bed. The living room was quiet and Landon found Ashley staring at the photo ornaments they'd collected over the years.

"I feel Christmas most when I'm right here. Beside you." She smiled up at him and slipped her arms around his waist. "The ornaments Cole made when he was two years old. The photos of the kids through the years. It's like all the Christmases come together every year on our tree."

"Mmmm." Landon held her close. "I feel Christmas most with you. Wherever you are."

She looked deep into his eyes. "You think Amy's okay?"

"She seemed like it." He brushed the hair from her face. "Hey . . . has anyone ever told you? You have the most beautiful hair."

"I seem to remember a certain handsome gentleman telling me that." She felt her troubled heart lighten. "A few times, anyway."

"Well . . . that certain gentleman has an idea." Landon peered out the window. "Let's take a walk out back to the creek. While the snow's still falling."

Ashley loved this about Landon, the way he could take any moment and make it unforgettable. He'd done that since the beginning, back when he had first tried to make her fall in love with him.

Back when her stubbornness had nearly cost her the love of her life. How many times had she rejected his attempts to pursue her? All because she had thought he was too safe. The two of them always seemed to have a desperate kind of love now. The result of knowing how close they'd come to losing it all.

"Mmmm." She leaned up and kissed him. "A walk sounds perfect."

When they were bundled up, they set out, hand in hand through the fresh fallen snow. The full moon cast an iridescent light over the blanket of white. "It's as bright as day."

Landon looked up at the sky. "I've never seen a more beautiful snowfall."

"It's perfect." Ashley stayed at his side as they made their way down to the creek. Their favorite bench was covered in nearly a foot of snow, but Landon used his coat sleeve to brush it off so they could sit. "I love the quiet after it snows."

"Like God's giving all of creation a chance to simply breathe."

"And rest."

Ashley leaned against him and together they were quiet for a long moment. "I miss Erin . . . on days like this."

"Me, too." Landon turned slightly so he could see her. "She and Sam used to love that old Christmas tree farm. The way the kids would run ahead and take dibs on the best ones."

Deep below the surface of the snow there was the gentlest sound of the creek. Still running. Proof that life continued even in the dead of winter. "I keep saying I'm worried about Amy. That she's the reason I don't want to meet Kendra Bryant on Christmas Eve."

Landon was quiet, his eyes locked on hers.

"But it's more than that."

"I know." He pressed his gloved hand against her bare cheek. "It's not Amy you're afraid for. It's yourself."

"Yes." Tears blurred her eyes and she moved her scarf further up her face. She grabbed hold of his hand. "Erin and I were never very close. Not for so many years."

"Until the end."

"Right." Ashley leaned her head on Landon's shoulder. "To hear her heart beating in the chest of someone else." She looked up at her husband again. "I'm not sure I can take it. I might start crying and never stop. Not till New Year's Day."

Landon nodded. "I get that. Completely."

Ashley peered at the snow-covered barren branches. "Christmas is hard enough, you know? My dad should understand that."

"I do." Landon pulled her closer.

Despite the cold air, in his arms Ashley felt warm. "You don't think I'm wrong to miss out?"

"Not at all. It's your choice, Ash." He stood and she did the same. He turned and faced her and slid her scarf down with his hand. Then, like a scene from a movie, he kissed her. With the lights from the house dim in the background and the world still around them. "I love you, Ashley Baxter Blake."

"I love you, too." This time she let the kiss

linger. "How come you always understand me?"

"Because." He lifted her scarf back into place and smiled at her. "You're my other half. God gave you to me. My greatest gift."

Landon took her hand and they headed slowly back to the house. As long as she lived, Ashley would remember this moment. It was forever etched in their hearts and minds. A winter night when just the touch of his lips and the sound of his voice soothing her soul was all she needed.

God was with them. And no matter how great the losses of the past, everything was going to be okay.

It really was.

CHAPTER EIGHT

The Christmas show was two weeks away, and Connor wondered how Bailey and Brandon ever pulled off a single performance as directors. Practice that night was slated for seven o'clock. Ten minutes ago. And still all forty-five kids were racing around the auditorium.

Connor tried to imagine the night ahead. Bailey hadn't been feeling well, so Brandon had returned from his meetings in L.A., and tonight he was in charge of rehearsal. He took a spot at the center of the stage and did the special CKT clap. The one the kids instantly recognized as a sign for them to be quiet.

A laugh came from somewhere in Connor's memory. He had been on this very stage doing that very clap just a few blinks ago. At least it seemed that way. The boys and girls responded with the same clap and Brandon grabbed the nearest microphone.

"Okay, everyone find a seat in front of the stage! We only have six more rehearsals. Tonight has to count."

Maddie walked in just then and hurried to the seat beside Connor. Suddenly Brandon's words rang in his heart. Yes, tonight had to count. Maddie had definitely been keeping to herself. They hadn't talked since the awkward Thanksgiving call. He'd tried texting her a few times but she hadn't responded.

He hoped tonight would be different.

While Brandon talked about the order of events for the night, Connor's sister entered the auditorium from the back and took the seat on the other side of him. "Whoever named it morning sickness never carried a child." Bailey slumped in her chair. "If I run out, you'll know why."

Connor felt horrible for her. "Brandon doesn't need Maddie and me for the next fifteen minutes. We can get you something. Decaf, maybe?"

"I can't stomach it. Not for the last few weeks." She closed her eyes and then her face lit up some. "What about hot tea? Chamomile? Would you mind?"

"Not at all." Connor motioned to Maddie. "Come on. We have time if we hurry."

The Coffee Shop, a few doors down from

the theater, was a favorite downtown Bloomington spot for shoppers and theater-goers. Connor waited until they were outside before he slowed his pace and glanced at Maddie. "It hardly felt like I was back at school at all."

"You got home last night, right?"

"Yes." Connor hesitated. If he could only figure out what was wrong with her. "Finished my finals yesterday morning."

"How do you think you did?" She smiled at him, but she was definitely more guarded now. Whatever he'd done to upset her, apparently he'd overstepped his bounds.

"Pretty well. Half A's, half B's." He stayed at her side as they navigated the busy sidewalk. "What about you?"

"Same." She was quiet while he ordered Bailey's tea and then a coffee for each of them. They headed back and not till they reached the door of the auditorium did she stop and turn toward him. "I'm sorry. I haven't been answering your texts."

"No." Connor angled his head, trying to see past the walls she'd raised between them. "Is it something I did?"

She shook her head. "Not at all. It's me." Maddie tucked her blond hair behind her ear and stared at the ground. "I can't talk about it."

Connor thought he understood. "If it's another guy, I get it. I never even asked if you were dating someone."

"I'm not." She lifted her eyes to him. "I just can't date. It's my own thing."

Connor blinked. What? She couldn't date? He was going to ask her why, but when he caught the determination in her eyes he let it drop. Instead he held the door open for her. "Then we'll be friends." He smiled at her. "Fair enough?"

"Yes." Her eyes brightened, and for the first time that night, the walls around her heart seemed to lower a little. "Thanks, Connor. For understanding."

He didn't let his disappointment show. Like Bailey had said, Maddie was young. She was still in high school. Maybe somewhere down the road they might have a chance at something more.

This simply was not that time.

Inside the theater, Brandon had split the children into two groups. A dance instructor taught one group the steps to the opening number, while the CKT choir director worked to help the others learn the first song of the show.

Connor approached Brandon. "Where do you want us?"

"Here." He pointed to the front row of

seats. "Sit with Bailey and watch for stragglers." He pointed to a little boy who had strayed from the others in the dance group. He was hopping like a frog near the edge of the stage, completely oblivious to the instructor. Brandon walked toward the boy, glancing over his shoulder at Maddie and Connor. "Kids like that one."

Brandon took the lead. "Hey, buddy. You wanna get back with your group?"

Maddie stifled a laugh. "That would be me . . . dancing to my own beat at that age."

"You need the patience of ten teachers to pull this off." Connor looked at his sister. "Is it always like this?"

Bailey held the hot tea close to her face. "Every time. A few weeks before opening night I always think we should call the whole thing off."

"I can see why." Maddie seemed to spot another wayward little one. She walked up onstage and headed for the singers. "Hey there."

The little girl lifted her head. "I'm a sheep."

"Right." Maddie took her by the hand and led her back to her group. "And sheep need to sing the very best of all."

Connor watched, his heart beating faster than before.

"I see you." Bailey turned and smiled at him. "She's so good with the kids."

"She's beautiful." Connor sat next to his sister. "But she doesn't like me."

"What?" Bailey looked from the stage back to Connor. "That's not what I saw during auditions."

"Something's changed." Connor shrugged. "Which is maybe for the best. I'll be back at school after Christmas."

"I think we've talked about this before." Bailey gave him a wary look. "Your challenge, dear brother, is to figure out what's troubling her."

Connor let his eyes settle on Maddie once more. "Yes. That, for sure, is the challenge."

Maddie hated how she'd forced herself to pull away from Connor. But it was only fair. She wasn't going to date him, so there was no point leading him on. At least he was willing to be her friend.

Rehearsal that evening went better than she thought it might. Ninety minutes into the practice, the kids knew the first two songs and the dance moves to the opening number. At the end of the session, they ran through the songs again and Maddie raised her eyebrows in Connor's direction.

"I can't believe it." She shifted her look to

Bailey. "These kids are really getting it."

"They always do." Bailey smiled. "That's the fun of putting on a show. Especially so quickly like this one."

When rehearsal was over, Connor walked Maddie to her car. He didn't try to hug her like before. She understood. She had made herself clear, no matter how much it hurt.

Before she climbed into her car, Connor folded his arms. "You still praying for your Christmas miracle?"

Maddie hadn't thought about that for a few weeks. "It was more for my sister than me."

"Hmmm." He looked into her eyes, as if he were trying to see past the mystery. "Is she sicker? You said she had health struggles."

"No." Maddie remembered her mother's words. How God had already answered one prayer after another where her sister was concerned. "Actually . . . maybe Hayley has already gotten her Christmas miracle."

"Okay." Connor seemed to take his time. As if he appreciated this moment alone with her. "What about you, Maddie West? What about your Christmas miracle?"

"For me . . . it's more just knowing that God's there." She wasn't usually this honest. But something about Connor Flanigan's kindness made her open up more easily. "You know?"

"Definitely." Connor hesitated. "Tell you what. Can I pray for you now? That God will show you He's real? Sometime between now and Christmas?"

Maddie felt his warmth to the center of her heart. "Please."

Connor took her gloved hands in his, and for the sweetest few minutes ever, he prayed for her. That God would speak to her and that she would sense His presence in many ways. But most of all that He would make Himself real to her — sometime before Christmas.

With Connor's prayer lingering in her soul, Maddie had expected the night to be more relaxed now. If ever there would be a time when she didn't think about her guilt, this had to be it. But that wasn't how it played out at all.

As soon as she was in bed with the lights out, the images came at her full force. She was running inside the house, the one where the birthday party was held, and she was asking her daddy, "Where's Hayley? I can't find Hayley."

And her father was scrambling up from his chair and there on the floor was Hayley's life jacket. The life jacket she absolutely had to wear if she was out of the house for even a minute. That's what her mom had told them both when she left the party for work.

But now the life jacket was on the floor. And Hayley was gone.

Maddie rolled around in bed, but the memory wouldn't stop. It wouldn't let her go.

"Hayley!" Their father screamed her name. "Hayley, where are you?"

And Maddie ran behind her dad out to the backyard and there . . . there at the bottom of the pool . . .

"No! No, God! No!" Her father's shout echoed through Maddie's being — then, and every day since. "Hayley!"

And her father was diving into the pool with his clothes on, diving down to the deep end and sweeping Hayley into his arms. Swimming her up to the surface and out onto the deck.

She lay in a wet heap. Her body still. "Hayley!" Everyone was screaming her name now. The adults at the party, the other children. And Maddie. Especially Maddie.

"Hayley, wake up!" Maddie rushed to her daddy's side, but he held her back. "Go inside, Maddie. Go!"

By then sirens were screaming in the distance. Shrill and piercing, sirens that told

Maddie, even at five years old, the truth. This wasn't a dream. Hayley had fallen in the pool without her life jacket and now she wasn't breathing.

Her dad had told her to go inside, but Maddie hadn't obeyed him. While her father pressed Hayley's chest over and over, Maddie found a place at the side of the pool. There, halfway hidden in the bushes, she watched and cried and prayed. *Please, God . . . please bring her back to life. Please!*

And then there was a rush of feet and noise as paramedics ran into the backyard and they took over, doing CPR on Hayley's little body. That's when Maddie caught a glimpse of her baby sister that stayed with her still.

Hayley's mouth was open . . . her eyes, too. Her face was blue and she was dead. Hayley was dead. There was no way around it. And Maddie ran into the house and hid under her friend's bed. She stayed there for a long time until one of the mothers found her.

And every single image from that day still lived in Maddie's mind as vividly as if it had just happened. Torturing Maddie. Reminding her day after day, night after night, of the truth.

Hayley had drowned at that long-ago

birthday party because of her.

Because she hadn't kept an eye on her little sister.

That's why Maddie didn't dare let herself fall in love. Because Hayley might've been given a miracle, a second chance at life. But that didn't mean Hayley's life would truly ever be the way it should've been. She would never experience love or independence the way she should have.

When Maddie woke up the next morning, exhausted from the memories of the night, she was convinced all over again. If Hayley couldn't live a normal life, she wouldn't either.

Period.

CHAPTER NINE

December fifteenth was Erin's birthday.

Every year, without fail, John Baxter had brought flowers to his daughters on their birthdays. Even Erin. Even now. He got up early, went to the florist, and chose a dozen long-stemmed yellow roses. Erin's favorites.

Then he took a drive that was too familiar. A drive to the local cemetery. John parked and trudged through the snow to the series of gravestones. Elizabeth. Little Sarah. Sam and Clarissa, Chloe and Heidi Jo. And there next to her mother — John's youngest daughter, Erin.

As John leaned down, as he anchored the bouquet of yellow roses deep into the icy snow, he saw something. An envelope in a plastic Ziploc bag. Proof that he wasn't the first one here this morning.

And he wasn't the only one thinking of Erin today.

John picked up the bag and removed the

letter from inside. It was from Ashley and it simply read: *Happy Birthday, Erin. I know you're happy in Heaven. I'm sure of it. But down here we still miss you. Especially today. I love you, Ashley.*

The cold air stung John's eyes as he blinked away a layer of tears. Beneath her name, Ashley had written one more thing:

P.S. — I'm sorry about Christmas Eve. I just don't know that I can do it. Dad's right. It's probably what you would do. But then . . . you always were stronger than me.

"Ah, Ashley . . ." He folded the note, put it back in the plastic bag and slid it beneath the yellow roses. "My poor girl."

Her note made him think. He needed to make sure Ashley knew it was okay. Okay that she missed the Christmas Eve with Kendra Bryant. Because Ashley was right. Not all of them could handle such a meeting.

Especially so soon after Erin's birthday.

Later John and Elaine drove to Indianapolis to finish their Christmas shopping. He told Elaine about Ashley's note, how she had basically apologized for not being able to participate in Christmas Eve dinner.

"You need to talk to her." Elaine looked like she could cry. "It's one thing to meet with the woman. But if Ashley feels like that, how does Luke feel? The two of them need to hear from you, John."

He agreed, so on the way home that day — with their car full of Christmas gifts — John called Luke first, and then Ashley. He told both of them he was okay with the fact that they weren't joining in for the Christmas Eve dinner. And that he was sorry for putting them in the situation to begin with. "You're right to listen to your heart in this," he told each of them separately. "I wouldn't want you to feel like you were disappointing me. Or like Erin would be disappointed."

Luke's response came easily. "I get it, Dad. It's just not how I want to spend Christmas Eve." He still sounded somewhat tense about the situation. But John understood. He knew Luke would be fine come Christmas morning.

The call with Ashley wasn't as simple. Her tone was sharp from the beginning. "Dad, you don't understand. I guess I figured you'd care more about what I want than what some stranger wants."

"I care deeply about you, Ash." John cast Elaine a frustrated look. "You can't really mean that."

"I do mean it. You chose her over us."

"I didn't choose her over . . ." John released a shaky breath. "I only wanted to reach out to her. Please . . . try to understand."

Ashley was quiet for a few seconds. "What about Amy? How could you be okay with bringing this woman into our family when you know it's going to hurt her? And me and Luke? At least the three of us."

John thought about disagreeing. They still didn't know for sure about how Amy would feel. She might be glad to meet Kendra. Now they'd never know. He kept his thoughts to himself. "I don't want to fight about it."

Ashley didn't respond at first. When she finally did, she sounded like she was crying. "I don't want to fight either. I'm sorry for getting so upset."

"No. Don't be sorry. The whole thing is my fault." John gripped the steering wheel. There was no way to make things right without letting Kendra down. And what sort of Christian example would that be? "Forgive me, Ashley. I really thought you'd want to be there."

"No way." She hesitated. "I'm curious. But, Dad, on Christmas Eve? I think I'd cry for a week."

When the call was over, just as they reached Bloomington again, John turned to Elaine. "I wish I could undo the whole

129

thing. Like Luke said, we could've planned to meet her after the new year."

Elaine took hold of his hand. "But for some reason God led you to make the plans now. At Christmastime." She settled back into her seat. "You did the right thing by calling them. You need to pray that God will show you why it was important to meet Kendra now."

"True."

"My guess is . . . this has a lot more to do with her than with any of the rest of us, John. Even you."

They were the exact words John needed to hear. God called His people to think of others first. That's all John had been trying to do by inviting Kendra over. Now they'd all have to find a way to get through the next few weeks.

Even if Christmas wasn't going to be the same because of it.

Kendra had received the package in the mail a week ago. An early Christmas present, from John Baxter and his wife, Elaine. The gift was a Bible study about the family of Jesus. In his card, John explained that there was no time like Christmas to get to know Jesus and His family.

Even for someone who had never believed

in God before.

This Saturday morning, days before Christmas, Kendra was snuggled under a blanket a few feet from the tree, completely caught up in the book. Moe was downstairs cleaning the garage.

Kendra ran her thumb over the cover of the book. Funny, how she had never thought about the family of Jesus. Probably because she had never thought much about Jesus, Himself. But in the last few days, she was touched at the possibility of Mary being visited by an angel and being told she was going to give birth to the Savior of the world. God in the flesh, wrapped in a blanket, safe in her arms.

With her heart defect, Kendra had long since given up the idea of having a baby — though at one time it had been her lifelong dream. But if she could have a child, if she gave birth to a son, she could hardly imagine seeing him born — only to be chased by wicked kings and discredited by a band of religious leaders and then finally, as a young man, to die on a cross.

As she read, Kendra could feel herself opening up a little more to the possibility. She couldn't help but think her mother would've liked the book. What if the Christmas story was more than a nice fable? More than a reason to decorate a tree and sing pretty songs and wrap presents?

Kendra wasn't finished yet but every page captivated her. Especially the story of Joseph. The Bible wasn't something Kendra had ever read, of course. But she knew enough about Joseph that his story spoke to her. Here was this guy who never expected any of the craziness that came with being engaged to Mary. He had to believe that his fiancée hadn't cheated on him, had to stand up to public ridicule. Then once baby Jesus was born, Joseph had to keep him safe by fleeing with his family again and again.

Joseph must've loved Mary more than life itself. That's what Kendra had always wanted from Moe. A devotion that would go the distance when life got tough.

When the book first arrived, Moe had spotted it on the kitchen counter. "What's this?" He'd held it up, his brow wrinkled.

"A gift. From John Baxter."

"Kendra." Moe had released a ten-ton sigh. "It's not normal. Your friendship with that family."

"Of course it's not normal." Kendra had refrained from raising her voice. "I'm alive because of their loss. But maybe I'm supposed to get more than a heart from them."

Moe had given her a look that was more

sympathetic than understanding. "Like what? A new understanding of life? Some kind of faith in God?"

"Maybe." Kendra had held her ground. "Things happen for a reason. I've always believed that."

Moe had flipped through the pages and then after a few seconds tossed the book back onto the kitchen counter. "They should've told you the heart came with strings attached."

"Moe!" Kendra still remembered the sting of his comment. "That's a terrible thing to say."

He had rolled his eyes and stormed out of the room. In the moments that followed — for the first time in her life — Kendra did something she had never done before.

She prayed. Or at least she talked to God. For the first time it occurred to her that the two were one and the same.

Not quite sure to Whom she was talking, Kendra had looked out the window and whispered her prayer out loud. "God, if You're real . . . if You're listening . . . could You soften Moe's heart, please? Our marriage is a mess right now, and truthfully . . . I don't think we're going to make it. But if You're there, and if You're real . . . then You can do anything. Even this." She had paused. "Anyway, it couldn't hurt to ask. Sincerely, Kendra Bryant."

At first, Kendra didn't notice anything different. If anything, she felt a little foolish. Because what good could come from talking to the air?

But then . . . a few hours later, after she'd long forgotten her prayer, the wildest thing happened. Out of the blue, Moe came home between tax planning appointments and found her reading the book. He helped her gently to her feet, took the book and set it down on the couch. "I'm sorry, Kendra. My attitude earlier, it was completely uncalled for."

Kendra had practically fallen back to her seat. She had wanted to tell him she agreed, that his words had hurt her and made her feel distant and alone. But she was so surprised — and so thankful — she could only listen.

Then, Moe had looked straight at her. The way he used to . . . like he still loved her. What he said next had stayed with her to this day. "Your surgery was like a turning point for us. The worst kind, and I can't figure out why." He ran his hand over her dark hair. "You came home from the hospital and ever since it seems all we do is fight."

"I know." She had looked down at the

place where their feet came together, her voice barely more than a whisper. "I hate it."

"I hate it, too." With the softest touch, Moe had lifted her chin so their eyes met again. "It's my fault. All of it."

"Work's been hard for you." Kendra had felt the stirrings of compassion toward him. "This time of year is always rough." The love in his eyes had felt wonderful. "And you've been worried about me. That's part of it."

"No. There's no excuse." His eyes had held hers. "Anyway, I'm sorry. You deserve better."

"Thank you."

He had picked up her book and handed it to her. "God isn't real. We both know that. But if you want to read the book, that's fine. It was a thoughtful gift. And Christmastime is for sharing nice thoughts." Then he'd kissed her lips, tenderly, in a way that took her breath. "No matter what you believe about God."

Every day since then, Moe had been kinder. More willing to talk about Kendra's feelings, her interest in Jesus and His family. Her curiosity about John Baxter and Erin's siblings. Like he'd undergone a different sort of heart transplant.

The memory lifted. Kendra closed the book and set it on the floor. She stretched her legs out on the sofa and propped her head on the arm. The tree was more beautiful this year. Or maybe Christmas was more beautiful. She put her hand on her chest and felt the steady beat. The pulsing rhythm that kept her alive and whole.

The heart that had once beat in the chest of Erin Baxter Hogan.

What had she been like?

Kendra replayed the details she knew. She'd looked her up on Facebook when she first found out the young woman's name. Her family had left her page up. Forever frozen in time the day before the accident.

Erin had been a wonderful mother and a happy wife. She and her husband were killed in the wreck, along with three of their four daughters. The one who survived now lived with her aunt and uncle in Bloomington. Part of John Baxter's extended Baxter family.

But beyond that, Kendra knew nothing. She could only wonder.

Something she didn't talk about with Moe or her doctor or anyone else was the fact that she felt different since the surgery. Kinder. More calm. More aware of relationships at a deeper level. She closed her eyes.

Was that possible? Had she gotten more than a piece of flesh and blood when she got Erin Baxter Hogan's heart? Was there some other aspect of Erin's soul that had crossed over, also?

Kendra breathed deep and sat up. She needed to finish the dishes and wrap a few gifts. Presents she had bought for John Baxter, and Erin's siblings. And little Amy. Erin's surviving daughter. Moe didn't know she'd spent money on the gifts yet. But she had a feeling he wouldn't be angry with her. Even though finances were tight.

Because for no earthly explanation, Moe had truly changed.

His apology that afternoon had stayed with him, and now it seemed he looked for ways to help her. He talked to her about her growing energy and her fears about whether her body would reject the heart. Sometimes he simply sat beside her and listened to her. The change was so great, so unexplained, that Kendra could only attribute it to one thing: the prayer she'd uttered that hopeless day a week earlier. Every day since then Kendra had pondered the other reality. There could be only one reason why her prayer had worked. A possibility Kendra hadn't fully grasped — even though she thought about it constantly.

The possibility that not only was Christmas the most wonderful time of the year.

It might also be true.

As true as the God who — just maybe — really did love His people enough to come to earth that first Christmas morning.

Even for an atheist like Kendra Bryant.

CHAPTER TEN

Connor had prayed for a Christmas miracle for Maddie every day since they met. But instead of seeing her grow happier and more sure of her faith as Christmas approached, Connor watched her slip a little further away. Now it was the Sunday before Christmas, the day of their show, and Maddie almost seemed like a stranger.

They gathered in the auditorium two hours before doors opened to run through the performance a final time. Maddie was onstage, helping the littlest children remember their places.

In the empty seating area, Connor took the spot next to Bailey and for a long moment he said nothing. Just watched her. Maddie had a beautifully tender way with the children — especially the littlest ones. Those who needed extra help.

The truth Connor couldn't escape was this: Maddie took his breath away more now than when they first met. And that night in the parking lot when he had prayed for her, Connor had hoped they still had a chance. But whatever had changed between them, Maddie was not interested. Not at all. Not even in being friends.

"What happened between you two?" Bailey looked pale as she glanced at him. She'd been chewing organic ginger candy all morning. She said it helped her nausea. "Maddie seemed so friendly at first."

"Maybe you could ask her." Connor was out of options. "I've tried talking to her and praying for her. She told me she was asking God for a Christmas miracle this year. She's pretty much avoiding me now. Like I've personally done something to upset her."

"No." Bailey watched Maddie, laughing with three of the little girls onstage. "She's not upset. That's not it. She's distant."

"Exactly." Connor sighed.

"Mostly with you." Bailey turned to him. "Maybe I'll talk to her."

"I wish you would. After the show, we'll probably never see each other again."

Bailey patted Connor's knee. "That's not true. She lives here. You're bound to run into her."

"I never ran into her before."

Bailey smiled at him. "You have her

number now. That should make a difference."

"I guess." Connor thought about that. Even a year from now he could text her randomly to see how she was doing. Maybe they could catch up and she'd be friendlier. The way she was the first time they met.

Bailey stood and made her way up onto the stage next to Brandon. Connor could see she wasn't feeling well. But he knew this was Bailey's favorite day of all. Opening night. The approaching showtime seemed to bring a rush of energy — not just to her, but to all of them.

Connor followed her up onto the stage and took his place near Maddie. He leaned close to her. "They're going to do great."

"I can't believe how far they've come." She smiled, but her eyes never quite met his.

Up front, Brandon had a quick conversation with Bailey. Then he turned to the group. "Okay, now who remembers the message of our show today?"

Several of the kids raised their hands. Brandon pointed to one little boy. "RJ?"

"Don't pick a bad Christmas tree!"

A few of the kids snickered. Connor met Brandon's and Bailey's eyes, the three of them working hard to keep straight faces.

Brandon took a step closer to the group. "It's something more than that. Who else wants to tell us?"

More hands filled the air. Bailey pointed to a little girl in the front row. "Janessa?"

The girl was only four. One of the youngest in the show. She was the daughter of Ashley Baxter Blake — a local artist who designed sets for most of the CKT shows, including this one. Connor remembered her. Their families got together every year or so.

Janessa smoothed the wrinkles from her dress and straightened herself. "For unto you is born this day a Savior . . . which is Christ, the Lord."

Bailey's eyes filled with tears, and Connor watched her and Brandon exchange a look. Connor understood. This would be them soon, parents of a precious child like Janessa. Bailey nodded, taking a moment, probably, to find her voice. "Yes, Janessa. That's exactly right. *A Charlie Brown Christmas* is about Jesus being born for all of us."

"Okay." Brandon put his arm around Bailey. "Let's run the show once more from the top."

Connor and Maddie stayed at the back of the group, helping children remember their cues and whether to walk off stage right or left when their numbers were finished. Again, Maddie was friendly but distant. Once, when their arms brushed against each other, Maddie practically jerked away. "Sorry."

"It's okay." Connor made a point to give her more space. Whatever was wrong, she wanted nothing to do with him. When the auditorium doors opened — thirty minutes before the show started — Connor found her backstage getting water.

"Hey." She opened a bottle and took a long sip.

"Maddie . . . did I do something to upset you?" Connor uttered a laugh, but it held no humor whatsoever. "I keep thinking back to the first few times we hung out, that time over coffee. I get you don't want to date. But now . . . it's like you don't want to be friends, either. What's going on?"

"Nothing. Really." Her answer was quick. "I need to help the girls in the first number."

She got a text at the same time, checked her phone and hurried off. Whatever was happening in Maddie's heart, Connor was convinced she wasn't being quite honest. Because as she turned away a single tear fell on her cheek. Connor watched her go and lifted his eyes to the theater rafters. *Help me here, Lord . . . I'm at a loss. Completely.*

There was no loud answer, no booming voice to tell him what to do. So Connor did what he needed to. He moved to his group of young actors and reminded them once more what to do when they got onstage.

This was why he was here — to help the kids. Tomorrow the show would be over and he would do what he obviously had to do next.

Put Maddie West behind him.

Maddie received the text from her mother as soon as the theater doors opened. Her parents and Hayley were picking up their tickets from the will call window. *Come find us,* her mother's second text read. *Hayley has someone she wants you to meet.*

Maddie stared at the text a moment longer. Someone Hayley wanted her to meet? Maddie hurried through the side door into the seating area and scanned the room for her family. Almost at the same time she spotted her mom and dad. Already the theater was crowded, so it was impossible to see Hayley and whoever Maddie was supposed to meet.

She moved through the crowd to the back right side of the auditorium, where her family was seated. Then, four rows from reaching them, Maddie felt her breath catch in her throat.

Hayley was sitting next to a boy her age.

For a few seconds, Maddie stopped and stared. Hayley's blond hair was curled and she wore a pretty red sweater and new dark jeans. Maddie continued pressing her way past the milling crowd and as she got closer she could hear her sister's happy voice. And Maddie could see something else.

Her sister was wearing makeup.

Not too much, but just enough that one thing was very clear. Hayley had a crush on the boy sitting next to her. Maddie reached her mother first and hugged her. When their faces were close, Maddie whispered, "What in the world?"

Her mom didn't answer. Instead, she motioned to Hayley and the boy. "This is Patrick. He's a friend from Hayley's class." She paused. "This is Hayley's sister, Maddie."

Immediately Patrick was on his feet. "Hello." He held out his hand. "Nice to meet you. Hayley says you're her best friend in the whole world."

"Yes." Maddie fought to keep herself from bursting into tears. "She's . . . she's my best friend, too."

"See?" Hayley giggled as she stood and hugged Maddie. Then in a voice not quite soft enough, she said, "Isn't he cute?"

Maddie nodded. "Yes." She smiled at Patrick and then at Hayley. "He's very nice."

"Hi, Maddie." Her dad stood then and kissed her cheek. "We're excited about the show. You all have worked so hard."

"Yes." Maddie felt dizzy from this revelation about Hayley. She forced a smile in her mother's direction. "Could you talk to me for a minute in the lobby?"

"Of course." Her mom motioned to the others. "I'll be right back."

When they were far enough away not to be heard, Maddie put her hands on her hips and paced one way and then the other. "Mom! You let Hayley bring a boy?"

"Of course." Peace shone from her mother's eyes. "They like each other. Why not bring him?"

"They *like* each other?" Maddie felt like she'd fallen into some unthinkable dream. "Are you serious? Hayley can't . . . She's . . ."

"She's what?" Her mom's expression grew deeper. "Do you think Hayley won't fall in love someday, Maddie?"

"No. I thought . . ." People were streaming past them, finding their seats. Maddie was careful to keep her tone from sounding too shocked. "I thought she would never have . . . what other people have."

Her mom looked back at their row of seats and then once more at Maddie. "Patrick suffered a brain injury at birth. He has strength where Maddie has weaknesses. And vice versa." Her smile seemed as much for herself as for Hayley. "They've been friends for several weeks now."

And Maddie had missed it. She'd been so caught up in punishing herself that more than a month had passed since she'd really talked to Hayley. Since she'd listened to how her sister was doing or whether she had made any new friends. Or whether she had a crush on a tall, handsome boy named Patrick.

"We can talk more later." Her mother kissed her forehead. "For now . . . just be happy for your sister."

"I will be." Maddie blinked back tears. "I am." She had to get backstage before the show started. She waved at her dad and Hayley and Patrick as she hurried down the aisle, through the door, and backstage with the others.

Connor Flanigan was one of the first people she spotted. And though they each had work to do, she went to him and took brief hold of his hand. "I'm sorry," she whispered near his face. "I have to talk to you. After the show. If you have time."

He searched her eyes, clearly confused. "Okay. I can do that."

She smiled. "Good."

And with that, the houselights went dark and the music began.

Maddie worked one side of the stage wings, while Connor worked the other. Between numbers, her eyes connected with his several times. How could she have treated him so badly? He was praying for her to have a Christmas miracle, and now God had given her one.

Hayley liked a boy!

The very thing Maddie expected would never be possible was happening. And if her mother's reaction was any indication, this was only the beginning for Hayley. One day she might actually fall in love and get married. Something Maddie had never thought could happen.

But along the way, she had taken her guilt and shame out on Connor. The more she was around him, the more she liked him. And the more guilty she felt because she had promised herself she would avoid falling in love. At all costs.

For Hayley.

The third number was wrapping up and Maddie watched Connor motion for a group of kids to exit the stage in his direction. So far they had no major mess-ups, nothing but the most adorable show. Everything was turning out to be exactly what they had worked so hard for.

Maddie's eyes met Connor's again. He smiled, like last time. But his confusion was clear all the way across the stage. Even once she tried to explain herself to him, she wouldn't blame him if he didn't want to see her again. She had shut him out completely. Even when he took the time to ask her if he'd done anything wrong. After this he would probably lose all interest in her.

The audience was clapping wildly over a song by three of the littlest girls — including Maddie's cousin Janessa. Out in the audience, Maddie spotted her aunt Ashley and uncle Landon as they cheered for their daughter. And between them another one of Maddie's cousins — Amy Hogan — raised both her hands, clearly thrilled for Janessa's performance.

Amy's parents should be here, God. Maddie closed her eyes for a quick moment. Chloe and Heidi Jo would've probably been on the stage right next to Janessa. When the number ended Maddie blinked her eyes open, and motioned for the girls to exit toward her.

"You did so good!" Maddie whispered to the cousins, hugging each of them. She watched them bounce and link arms and celebrate the success of their song. As they walked away, a thought hit Maddie. The losses in the Baxter family were many, but maybe God really was still with them.

Otherwise how could she explain a day like this?

Not until the show was over did Maddie realize Connor was gone. She got a text from him while she was cleaning up with a crew of parents and older kids.

Sorry! Bailey wasn't feeling good, so I took her home. I guess we'll have to talk some other time.

Maddie read the text and felt the disappointment deep within her. Her fingers flew across the phone's keyboard. *No problem. Maybe we can get together after Christmas. I still want to talk.*

His next text took a few minutes. *Sure. Sounds good. Great job tonight.*

She had hoped he would ask her to meet sooner. Tomorrow or the next day. But she understood. After how she'd acted, Maddie could hardly blame him. She typed out her final text. *Thanks. You too.* Then she slipped her phone into her purse and set about her work.

The trouble with Connor was all her fault. She could've at least explained her situation, helped him understand how she felt about Hayley. Now he was probably glad to have a reason to leave early.

A realization hit Maddie as she drove home, as she thought about the amazing performance by the kids and how she'd lost her chance with Connor Flanigan. Something that brought comfort despite her disappointment. God really had given her the Christmas miracle she had prayed for.

His name was Patrick.

And that was enough. Maddie smiled as she pulled into her neighborhood.

No matter how Christmas turned out for her.

CHAPTER ELEVEN

The worst snowstorm of the year descended on Indiana late in the afternoon the day before Christmas, making John thankful for three things. First, that they had all gone to the four o'clock Christmas Eve service that afternoon at Clear Creek Community Church. Second, that Kendra Bryant had decided to come early. Already she had texted John to say she was in town, doing some last-minute shopping near the university.

And finally, John was thankful that Luke and Reagan and the kids had decided not to come.

In John's perfect picture of the day, all of his family would be together to meet Kendra. But with the severity of the storm he could only thank God that Luke and Reagan would be safe at home. Already local news was warning people to cancel plans and stay off the interstate.

Ashley helped Elaine with the cooking, even though Ashley and her family weren't going to stick around for dinner. They had planned to spend Christmas Eve with Landon's family several hours away. But the storm changed everything and instead, Landon had made reservations at their favorite nearby steak house.

John found them in the kitchen. He approached Ashley and put his hand on her arm. "You sure about dinner? We could move the party to Brooke's house so you all could stay here. Brooke's only a few miles away."

"Dad, really. We're fine." Her eyes held an acceptance that hadn't been there before. "We told the kids we'll take them to a movie after dinner. Everyone's okay with the plan."

Dinner tonight would be stuffed chicken and roasted vegetables. Ashley was saving the turkey for tomorrow when the entire family would be together. As long as Luke and Reagan could get out from the storm.

When the dinner was ready, Elaine thanked Ashley. "I'll keep it in the oven till everyone gets here."

John moved into the kitchen. "I'm sorry again, Ashley." He took the spot next to Elaine. "We should've had it in January."

"It's okay." She hugged him and their eyes

held. "Let me know how it goes."

"I will."

Ashley went upstairs to get ready. Landon was already up there helping the kids wrap presents.

Christmas music filled the house, but it did nothing to dim the regret in John's heart. He turned to Elaine. "I've been thinking about something."

She put her hand on the side of his face. "Tell me."

"The last thing I wanted to do this Christmas was divide everyone."

"I know." Her tone was understanding, but it didn't change the truth.

John stared out the window at the snow-covered garden behind the house. The one he'd planted three decades ago. Wasn't it yesterday when Erin and her sisters played hide-and-seek in that garden? A sigh slid from John's heart. "This dinner with Kendra Bryant . . ." John's eyes found Elaine's again. "The first time I heard Erin's heartbeat she was just seconds old. The doctor laid her in my arms."

"John."

He nodded. His eyes shifted to the backyard again. "She was our fourth little girl, but she had her own way. A happy, gentle spirit that defined her . . ." He smiled at

Elaine. "Till the day she died."

Elaine's eyes looked damp. "I always loved Erin."

"But that heartbeat, the one unique to my youngest daughter, that's what this is about." He looked intently at Elaine. "Right?"

"It's more than that."

"I know, but I want to hear it. My baby girl's heartbeat." John took a step back. "All of this . . . it's for me. Which makes me wonder, Elaine. It does."

"I'm sorry."

John turned and slowly walked toward the front porch. "Come sit with me. For a few minutes."

Elaine followed him and they grabbed their jackets on the way outside. John brushed a fine layer of snow off the porch swing and then he took hold of Elaine's hand as they sat down. Snow was coming down hard, swirling in the wind. But they stayed dry where they were sitting.

John sighed. "I care about Kendra. I do. But it's Christmas Eve."

"And you want to hear your daughter's heartbeat one more time." Elaine laid her head on his shoulder.

"Exactly."

She turned so she could see him. "It's

okay. The kids understand." Her voice remained calm. "Don't you think they feel the same way, John? Deep down?"

That hadn't occurred to him. After all, he'd presented the meeting with Kendra as something Erin would've wanted, something good for Kendra. A chance to open her life to the possibility of faith.

A feeling of peace came over him. Peace he hadn't felt in weeks. Maybe Elaine was right. "So you think the real reason Kari and Brooke and Dayne are willing to be here is because . . . it'll feel like we have Erin back. For one night, anyway?"

"I think that's part of it."

"Hmmm." John nodded. "Thank you." He eased her into a hug. "Do me a favor."

"Anything."

"Pray for me. That I'll care about Kendra, as a person. That this will be about more than hearing Erin's heartbeat."

"I will. I'll pray all night."

"Thank you." He breathed deeply. "I feel good about that." He stood and helped Elaine to her feet. "Let's go make dessert. It's freezing out here. And we have less than an hour until everyone shows up."

With that, John and Elaine went inside and the two of them made a baked apple crumble and fresh whipped cream for after dinner. John stopped at the window and stared outside again. He was going to be okay. He cared about Kendra Bryant, he truly did. Tonight would be about her, not Erin. But deep down, Elaine had helped him understand that he was normal to hold on to one very real thing.

The fact that tonight — for the first time in years — he would have a part of his daughter Erin back again.

They'd been home from church for an hour when Luke Baxter asked his wife, Reagan, to meet him in their bedroom. She had been helping little Johnny get dressed for dinner at their favorite restaurant.

"I think I made a mistake." Luke sat on the edge of their bed. "I feel like we should be there tonight. At Ashley and Landon's house."

Reagan sat beside him, confusion clouding her eyes. "I thought you didn't want to go. Because of that Kendra woman."

"I don't. Not really." He faced her. "But Tommy asked me this morning if it was really true. If we weren't going tonight." Luke felt sick about the situation. "He said the Baxter cousins look forward to Christmas Eve dinner all year."

Reagan took a few seconds, but then she

nodded. "That's true. They do."

"I should've changed my mind earlier." He shook his head. "I've been so busy on the case at work, I didn't take time to think about it. To talk to you and the kids and make a right decision."

Outside the wind howled. The snowstorm forecast to cover Indiana was just hitting. Reagan glanced out the window. "Looks like the weather may have made the decision for us."

"Nah." Luke walked across the room and peered outside. "We've driven in snowstorms before."

Reagan was quiet. "This is about your mom, isn't it?"

For a long beat, Luke stayed by the window, staring into the stormy night. When he turned around, he felt tears in his eyes. "Maybe. Deep down." He came to Reagan and pulled her into his arms. "She would've wanted us all together."

"True." Reagan put her hands against his cheeks. "What about Ashley?"

"Could you text her? Just so she knows we're coming. It's the right thing to do. For our family, for my dad." He smiled. "Let's go tell the kids."

Luke thought about his decision as the kids celebrated the news. He still couldn't understand his father wanting Kendra Bryant to be part of their evening. The woman would never be family — even if she did have Erin's heart. But her presence didn't change the fact that it was Christmas.

And Christmas was for family.

Twenty minutes later, despite the raging storm outside, Luke and Reagan, Tommy, Malin, and Johnny were piled in the car and headed from Indianapolis to Bloomington. Fifty miles and they'd be where they always were on Christmas Eve — blizzard or not. The home where Luke had been raised. The one his sister and her husband now owned.

The Baxter house.

CHAPTER TWELVE

The text came through while Ashley was upstairs in the bathroom getting ready for dinner in downtown Bloomington. They were about to clear out so the Baxter family Christmas Eve party could happen where it always did. At her house. Landon had just announced that they were five minutes from leaving, and already the kids were gathered in Cole's room.

Ashley set down her curling iron and picked up her phone. The message was from Reagan. *We're headed to Bloomington. Luke changed his mind. He says maybe your mom would've wanted us to all be there.*

A sick feeling wrapped itself around Ashley as she rattled off a quick response. *Are you serious? So you're already headed here?*

Yes. Luke's driving. He says it's Christmas. And the old Baxter house is the only place we want to be.

Ashley texted back. *What about the storm?*

According to Luke, he's driven through worse. Pray for us.

A long sigh came from the broken places in Ashley's heart. How could Luke change his mind at the last minute? Especially when he was so set against the meeting with Kendra. And how could her family be the only ones not here tonight? She leaned against the bathroom wall and closed her eyes. *God, what are we supposed to do?*

"Honey?" Landon came to her and took hold of her hands. "Everything okay?"

She held up her phone. "Reagan just texted. She and Luke and the kids are headed here. They changed their minds."

Landon's expression showed no sign of surprise. His eyes looked deeper than Lake Monroe. "You only get so many Christmases."

"I know." Tears stung at her eyes. "Maybe we need to explain things to the kids. See what they think. Ask them their opinion."

A smile tugged at the corners of Landon's lips. "I like that idea."

"You know." Ashley linked her arms around his neck and hugged him. "I should've thought about that sooner."

"At least you're thinking about it now." Landon kissed her lips. "I'll go get them."

The meeting took place on Ashley and

Landon's bed. Where they often had talks with their kids. Landon took the lead.

"Your mom and I have something to ask you."

Ashley watched as Devin raised his hand and began talking. "Is it about why we're leaving our own house for Christmas Eve?" He sat cross-legged at the center of the bed. "Because that's what us kids were talking about in Cole's room. Plus, Pastor said Christmas is for getting along with people."

"It's true." Cole shrugged, his expression guilty. "I mean, none of us really get it."

"That's my fault." Ashley thought about the pastor's message from earlier that day. Devin was right. Pastor Atteberry talked about giving people grace and making an effort to think of others first. She sighed and knelt on the bench at the end of their bed so she could face the children. "I made a decision about tonight I thought was best." She paused, looking at each of their precious faces. "But now I'm not sure I was right."

"It's about that lady, right?" Amy's voice was quieter than the boys', her face marked by sadness.

"It is, Amy. That's right." Landon came up alongside Ashley. "A special guest is joining the family for dinner tonight at our house. Her name is Kendra Bryant."

All this time Ashley had believed that the kids knew nothing about the details. She and Landon had kept the information from them so Amy wouldn't get upset.

But now Ashley was sure she was wrong. At the mention of the woman's name, Amy stared at the bedspread. Tears spilled from her blue eyes and onto her cheeks.

Ashley slid onto the bed between Amy and Janessa. "You know about Kendra Bryant?"

"Yes." Amy's voice was barely more than a whimper. "She has my mommy's heart."

The words hit Ashley like a series of blows to her gut. She looked over her shoulder at Landon and then back at Amy. "Yes. That's right."

"Why, Mommy?" Janessa took hold of Ashley's hand. She was only four but the conversation clearly was making her nervous. "Why did someone take her mommy's heart?"

Ashley felt Landon's hand on her shoulder. His presence gave her strength. "Okay . . ." She looked from Janessa to Amy, and then to the boys — Cole and Devin. "You all know that Amy's family went home to heaven."

"Because of the car accident." Devin looked at Landon. "A truck hit their van, right, Daddy?"

"That's right." He put his finger to his lips. "Let Mommy finish."

"Okay." He lifted concerned eyes to Ashley. "Sorry."

"Thank you, Devin." Ashley searched for the words. "Anyway, when Amy's family went to heaven, her mommy gave her heart to another woman. The woman's name is Kendra Bryant."

"Doesn't she need a heart in heaven?" Devin raised his brow, clearly concerned. "Is it okay if I ask that?"

"Of course." Ashley patted Devin on the back. "The answer is no. She doesn't need it. In heaven, Aunt Erin has a new heart."

"Oh." Amy nodded, fresh tears sliding down her cheeks. "I wondered about that."

Cole shifted closer to Amy and put his arm around her shoulders. "So we're not staying for dinner? Because of Amy? Because we don't want to meet Kendra Bryant?" He shrugged. "Sorry, Mom . . . Dad. Just trying to understand."

Amy was crying harder now. Ashley held out her arms to the girl. "Come here, honey." But Amy slid off the bed and ran out the door.

"Yes. That's why." Ashley gave Cole a sad smile. "Your dad and I thought it would be too hard for Amy."

Cole nodded. "I didn't know."

Ashley took a few steps toward the door. "Your dad and I thought it would be too hard for Amy."

"We're all trying to figure out the right thing to do." Landon nodded at Ashley. "Honey, you go talk to her. We'll stay here."

"We should pray for Amy, right, Daddy?" Janessa's eyes filled with compassion. "That's what I do when she gets sad."

"Yes, baby." Landon exchanged a look with Ashley. "We'll pray for her."

Ashley headed for the door. "I'll be right back."

Ashley fought her own tears as she hurried down the hall to Amy's room. Amy was lying on her bed, her face in her pillow. Her whole body shook from her tears.

"Amy." Ashley sat on the edge of her bed. "Sweetie, I'm so sorry. I never wanted any of this to upset you."

It took a few seconds, but eventually Amy rolled onto her back and then sat up. Her tearstained face hadn't looked this sad in a very long time. Ashley hugged the child close, running her hand over Amy's long blond hair. "We don't have to meet the woman. That's why we're going somewhere else for dinner. So you don't have to be sad."

165

"I . . . know. But . . ." The sobs still shook her little body. "What if . . . what if I want to meet her?"

Ashley drew a quick breath. What had her niece said? The floor might as well have fallen away. Ashley blinked and tried to exhale. "Amy . . ." Ashley slid back and searched the girl's eyes. "You want to meet her?"

Amy hung her head and nodded. When she looked up, the sadness in her eyes was almost too much for Ashley. "A long time ago . . ." Amy grabbed a few quick breaths, her tears subsiding a bit. "A long time ago I heard you and Uncle Landon talking . . . about meeting her. And I thought that would be nice."

"Honey, why didn't you tell us?" Suddenly her father's words at the tree farm that day came back to Ashley. All this time he had been right.

"You said you didn't want . . . to meet her." She wiped her eyes with the backs of her hands. "I didn't think I had a choice."

"Oh, Amy." Ashley held her close again. "You could've said something just then, during our meeting."

"I didn't want to change everyone's minds."

The situation was making sense to Ashley.

She felt the heaviness of Amy's heartache. "I should've asked you. I'm so sorry, honey."

Amy lifted her head and looked straight at Ashley. "You mean . . . you might stay here? If that's what I wanted to do?"

"Of course." Ashley's own concerns about meeting Kendra faded. "If you want to stay here, then we'll stay. And, honey, you can always tell us how you feel. We love you so much, Amy."

"Okay." She sniffed a few times. "It's just . . . I love Christmas with you and Uncle Landon. This is my home now." Her eyes watered again. "And you are my family. But . . . sometimes I miss Christmas the way it used to be. With Mommy and Daddy and my sissies." More tears rolled down her cheeks. "I thought maybe . . . maybe if I heard my mommy's heartbeat one more time . . . it would be the best Christmas of all."

"Well, then . . . we'll stay here tonight. And together we'll meet Kendra Bryant." Ashley reached for a tissue from the nightstand and wiped Amy's tears. How wonderful that they were having this conversation today and not tomorrow. When it would be too late. "And we *will* have the best Christmas of all." She kissed the top of Amy's head. "Okay?"

Amy smiled despite her teary eyes. "All of us together."

"Exactly." Ashley stood. "Why don't you wash your face, and I'll tell the others."

When she was on her feet, Amy paused for a moment and then ran into Ashley's arms. "I love you."

"I love you, too, honey." Ashley couldn't stop her own tears this time. If only Erin were here to hold her daughter and love her like this. If only the rest of her family were downstairs getting ready for Christmas.

The way it should've been.

"Aunt Ashley, can I tell you something?"

"Of course." She stooped down so she could look straight into Amy's eyes. "Anything."

"Sometimes at night, when you and Uncle Landon come in to say prayers, you look just like my mommy. And you sound like her."

Ashley hugged her once more. There was nothing she could say, no way to stop the tears that coursed down her cheeks. After a while, Ashley looked at Amy again. "Honey . . ." She dabbed at her tears. "I'm sure — from somewhere in heaven — that makes your mommy very happy."

The smile that filled Amy's face made Ashley sure everything was going to be okay.

Ashley went down the hall to her room and told the others the new plan. They were staying for dinner and meeting Kendra Bryant, after all.

Only then did Ashley realize how much her kids had wanted things to work out this way. Cole and Devin clapped and high-fived each other and Janessa danced circles around Landon.

When the kids were out of the room, Ashley told Landon what had happened, and how Amy loved being part of their family, but how hearing her mother's heartbeat would make this the most amazing Christmas. "I never would've imagined she might *want* to meet the woman." Ashley felt exhausted from the heartache of it all. "The way my dad suggested a month ago." She paused. "I'm so grateful, Landon. What if we would've just gone to dinner and never talked about it?"

Landon linked his arms around her waist and swayed with her for a long moment. "That's what makes you special, Ashley." He kissed her again. "You did talk about it."

Peace whispered to her soul. The same way it always did when she was with Landon. "Thank you."

The doorbell rang downstairs.

"That's our cue." Landon took her hand and led her to the bathroom. "Freshen up. I'll take the kids downstairs."

Ashley looked in the mirror and fixed the few places where her mascara had run. As she did, she thanked God again for her family, for kids who loved each other and for a husband who had been her greatest strength as far back as she could remember.

And for a Christmas Eve that would be difficult, for sure. But also — just maybe — a night that would be like Amy said.

The best Christmas ever.

CHAPTER THIRTEEN

John's heart beat hard inside his chest as he went to answer the door. After all the letter-writing and discussion, the meeting with Kendra Bryant was about to happen. But when he opened the door, instead of Kendra, Kari and Ryan stood on the doorstep.

"Merry Christmas, Dad!" Kari stepped up and hugged him. She was covered in snow, and she had to yell to be heard above the sound of the howling wind. "Is she here? Kendra?"

"Not yet." He felt his nerves relax a little. "Any minute, though."

Ryan hugged him then, and each of the kids did the same. They had bags of wrapped gifts and a plate of Christmas cookies.

"For Grandma Elaine." Jessie smiled. "Where is she?"

John loved this about his family, how they had adapted to heartache and tragedy over the years. Yes, all the kids and grandkids missed Elizabeth but each in their own timing and their own way, had taken Elaine into the family.

Jessie's cookies were proof.

Love like this was part of their story of redemption. No matter what happened, as long as they had each other, they would still be Baxters.

And they would be fine.

They headed to the kitchen where Brooke and Peter and their girls were helping Elaine set the two tables. Dayne and Katy and their kids would arrive in twenty minutes.

"Has anyone heard from Luke and Reagan?" Ashley was walking down the stairs with Landon at her side. "He should be here about the same time as Dayne and Katy."

The others stopped for a moment and looked at each other. John was the first to speak. "Luke's coming?"

"He didn't want to miss being with the whole family." Ashley paused at the bottom of the stairs and then crossed through the group to John. "We're staying, too, Daddy." She looked back at the kids. "You were right." She stared into his eyes. "Amy wanted to meet Kendra. So now we all want to meet her."

John couldn't believe it. Earlier today he

had been sure he'd made a mess of Christmas. And now . . . now they would have the Christmas Eve he'd prayed for. The one he'd dreamed about.

They all surrounded John for a group hug, just as his phone rang. He pulled it from his pocket. It was Luke. "Hello?"

"Dad!" The connection was fuzzy. "We're stuck in this snowstorm about twenty miles from Bloomington. Can't see a thing."

The warm feeling from a moment ago was immediately gone. "Are you safe? You and Reagan and the kids?"

The others gradually backed up, giving him space to talk.

It seemed like Luke had to yell to be heard. "We're safe for now in the car. But the traffic isn't moving. The way it's snowing . . . snowdrift." Static sounded over the line. Luke mentioned a mile-marker number. "We might . . . be stuck for a while."

John refused to acknowledge the panic that rushed at him. "Stay in the car. I'll make some phone calls." John wanted to get in his truck and find them. Instead he told Luke the family would pray.

The doorbell rang as John hung up the phone, his focus entirely on Luke and Reagan and the kids. Kari answered the door and there, standing outside in the snow, were Kendra Bryant and her husband, Moe. The man who wasn't supposed to join her. Whatever had happened between them he was here now.

"Hi." Kari was the first to step up and hug her. "You must be Kendra."

"Yes." She removed her snowy coat and the man beside her did the same. Ryan took both coats and hung them on a rack near the front door. Kendra looked at the man beside her. "This is Moe, my husband."

John hadn't been sure what Kendra would look like. He almost expected her to look like Erin. But she was taller, more slender with dark hair and pretty dark eyes. She looked younger than John had anticipated. And shaky, nervous.

As deep as his emotions were in this moment, hers had to be equally intense.

John stepped up to her. "Kendra." He took hold of her hands. "I'm John Baxter."

"Hi, John." And then it happened. The hug John had thought about for the last few years.

He didn't hold on too long, didn't want to make Kendra feel uncomfortable. But her heart was beating hard, and in that short embrace, he felt it against his chest. The heartbeat he had first felt when Erin was a baby. The one he felt on her wedding day, moments before he walked her down the aisle.

The steady, strong, beautiful heartbeat of his youngest daughter.

John stepped back, practically dizzy from the reality. Erin's heart was right here, in the same room with them. Ashley hugged Kendra next and then she introduced Kendra and Moe to the others.

When it came time for Amy's introduction, Ashley hesitated. "This is Amy."

Kendra seemed to know immediately that Amy wasn't like the other children. Her smile faded some. "Hello, Amy." The two of them remained several feet apart. "Maybe we can talk later, okay?"

"Okay." Amy clung to Janessa near the back of the group of kids. Her eyes were wide, like she was scared or maybe because she simply didn't know what to do next.

Ashley didn't let the moment become awkward. She continued through the room introducing each of her siblings, their spouses, and their kids.

"There's even more of us still coming," Cole added when Ashley reached the end. "But don't worry. We won't test you later."

Kendra laughed, and the sound seemed to give the others permission to relax. They'd gotten past the newness and strangeness of the situation. John hoped now they could enjoy the dinner celebration and focus on Christmas.

John felt Elaine come alongside him and put her arm around his waist.

She looked at the group. "Let's move into the kitchen. I have hot tea on the stove."

Katy and Dayne and their kids arrived a few minutes later and John held up his hand. "I just got a text from Luke. They're still stuck in the snow on the interstate. He asked if we'd pray for them."

John was sure everyone was struggling not to think about Erin and Sam's accident, how they had been stopped on the highway when a semitruck crashed into them. John refused to think about it. Instead, he held out his hands and with practiced ease the family circled up.

Kendra and Moe drew back, giving the family their space. John motioned to them. "You can join us. You're part of the family tonight."

The two of them looked at each other, and Moe made the first move, stepping slowly into the circle. Kendra did the same, and they waited, clearly unsure about what was happening.

"Hey! This reminds me of the Grinch cartoon." Devin whispered loud enough for most of them to hear. *"Christmastime is in our grasp . . . so long as we have hands to clasp."*

The boy's words held a wisdom that settled over the room. John led the prayer. "Lord, we ask you for a Christmas miracle tonight. That you would help Luke and Reagan and the kids find their way out of the snow. That they would feel Your presence right now, Father. Please rescue them, that they might be here where we are. And please keep them safe. In Jesus' name, amen."

John called the local highway patrol and asked about the safety of people stuck on the road. "All traffic is stopped," an officer told him. "We're doing our best to get to everyone, but the storm came up faster than we expected."

The information left John feeling anxious. But thirty minutes later, when they were getting settled at the two long tables in the dining room, the doorbell rang again. John felt his heart jump. But then, from outside on the doorstep, muffled by the blizzard, he heard the sound of singing.

"We wish you a merry Christmas, we wish you a merry Christmas, we wish you a merry Christmas . . . and a happy New Year!"

By the time John rushed to the door, half

his family had hurried in behind him. As he opened it, there was Luke, one arm around Reagan, the other around Malin. Tommy and Johnny stood on either side, and though the wind was blowing snow in their hair and onto their coats, they had never looked happier.

At the same instant, they switched up their song. Luke led the group. "We'll be home for Christmas . . . you can count on us!"

John pulled his son into the house and hugged him for a long time. "You're here!"

"It was the craziest thing." Luke took off his coat and hung it up, and the rest of his family did the same. "We were stuck in a snowdrift so high . . . I thought it might be two days before we got out."

"Definitely." Reagan's eyes showed the depth of her concern. "And then all the sudden this snowplow came from out of nowhere."

"This man gets out and knocks on Dad's window." Tommy was clearly still so excited about what happened, his words ran together.

Luke nodded. "Exactly. He told me his name was Jag. Interesting name, right? Anyway, he said he would clear the way for me, and to just trust him."

"You forgot the other part, Daddy." Malin

tugged on his shoulder. "About Jesus."

"Right." Luke shook his head. "That was the most amazing thing. First words he says when I opened the window were 'Do you believe in Jesus?' "

"We said, 'Yes, of course.' " Reagan locked eyes with Luke. "That's when the man said he was going to clear the way."

Luke went on to explain how the man plowed the shoulder so that Luke could get traction as he drove out of the snowbank. "After a few miles, the storm let up and the road ahead was clear."

"But we never saw where the snowplow went." Tommy looked at his cousins and then at Luke. "Right, Dad?"

"Right." Luke shrugged. "Like one minute we were following him through the thickest snow I've ever seen. And the next thing we know he's gone. Vanished."

Chills ran down John's arms. "When was that?"

Reagan checked the time on her phone. "Maybe thirty minutes ago."

For several seconds, the others just looked at each other. Kendra spoke first. "That's exactly when we held hands and prayed." She looked at Moe. "It was, right?"

"Definitely." Elaine checked her phone. "I texted Reagan after we prayed. It must've happened right after that."

Reagan had tears in her eyes. "God must've wanted us here. With all of you."

At that point, Luke took a few steps toward Kendra Bryant. "I'm Luke. Erin's youngest brother."

"I'm Kendra."

John watched, amazed at the change in Luke. He had definitely wanted to avoid a moment like this. But now here he was extending kindness to Kendra the way John had hoped.

"My dad told us Erin would've wanted this. For us to meet you and see for ourselves the difference her life meant."

"I believe that, too." For the first time since she walked through the front door, John watched Kendra blink back tears as she leaned against her husband. Then she looked around the room at the others. Each of them one at a time. "I was going to wait and say this later. When we open presents. But I need to say it now, before another minute passes."

John felt his throat tighten. He had known this moment was coming, and that it would be hard for all of them.

"A few years ago I got sick. My heart took the worst of my illness and there was no cure." She pressed in toward her husband.

"Without a new heart, I would be dead by now."

Two tears slid down John's face. Around the room he could see the others crying, too. Even a few of the older grandchildren. Standing across from Kendra, Ashley hugged Amy close.

Kendra continued. "But there was a problem. If I was going to live, someone else would have to die."

Moe cleared his throat. "She almost didn't put her name on the list. For that reason."

"I couldn't stand the thought that I might get to live, but someone else wouldn't." She looked at Moe. "Then my husband told me something I hadn't thought about before. People die. The death of a heart donor would happen whether I accepted a new heart or not." She shifted her look to John. "And he told me something else. If a person agrees to be an organ donor, then that's something very personal. Something that person chose to do."

"Yes." John dabbed at his eyes and nodded. "Erin was like that."

"So . . . what I wanted to tell you all is this." Tears filled Kendra's eyes, but her words came anyway. "I'm sorry about what happened to Erin. If I had to choose, I would've died so that *she* could live." Kendra looked at Ashley and Luke, Kari and Brooke and Dayne. Last of all she looked at Amy. "I absolutely would have." She hesitated. "But it doesn't work that way. And now . . . I'm here and she isn't. And I'm so sorry about that."

"It's not your fault." John stepped forward and took Kendra's hand. "We all know that."

"Yes." She caught a few tears with her fingertips. "But I wanted you to know how thankful I am. For this gift of life." She looked right at John. "I wish I would've known Erin. But because of you" — she looked around — "all of you, I feel like I do. So . . . thank you for that, too."

The moment was tougher than John had expected. But it was necessary. John took a deep breath. "Why don't we all go eat. And during dinner, maybe everyone can tell Kendra something they loved about Erin."

His family nodded and murmured their quiet agreement. As the group headed back to the table, John hoped he had made the right decision. They hadn't talked about Erin openly like this in a long time.

But it took only a few minutes for him to know that this was exactly what they needed. With Kendra here, they were all thinking about Erin and Sam and the girls.

This gave the family a chance to remember them. Especially Erin. Not just the kindness she showed to others, but the funny things she used to say and the way she made a family celebration warmer — just by being in the room.

"Back when we used to have a kids' table at Thanksgiving, Erin always sat with them." Brooke's eyes grew distant, her laugh drawn from days gone by. "Maddie and Hayley used to think she was one of the cousins."

Kari nodded. "I remember one Thanksgiving Jessie brought matching hair ribbons for all the little girls. Remember, the ones with purple turkeys on them?"

"Absolutely." John chuckled. He could picture his youngest daughter as clearly as if she were sitting there at the table. "Erin got one, too."

"Yes." Kari smiled. "She wore it all day."

They shared throughout dinner, and several times one of them remembered something that made the others laugh. Even Kendra's mood seemed lighter, she and Moe now more connected to the Baxter family.

After dinner and dessert they headed into the living room and gathered around the tree. They would be together again tomorrow, but tonight John had a gift for each of his grandkids — something special Elaine and he had chosen for each of them.

As the kids opened gifts, John noticed again that Amy was quieter than the others. She still hadn't had a moment with Kendra. Not like John had pictured. It made him wonder how Amy was taking all this.

When the children were finished exchanging presents, Kendra stood and brought a large bag into the room. "I have a few gifts, too."

"You didn't have to get us anything." John had already told her that during one of their phone calls. "We're just thankful you and Moe are here."

"Yes." She nodded. "I know. But . . . I wanted to." She pulled a gift from the bag and handed it to John. "This is for you and Elaine."

John's hands trembled as he took the present and set it between him and Elaine. He spoke softly to her. "You go ahead."

She slid off the wrapping paper and at the same time they both saw the gift. It was a wooden heart, made of rough-hewn older wood. And painted across it were the words "The Heart Remembers . . ."

Kendra watched him read it. "I'm different since the transplant." Her voice cracked as she spoke. "As if some of what mattered to Erin, now matters to me. Especially her faith."

Tears blurred John's vision. He handed the heart to Elaine and crossed the room to hug Kendra. He wanted to ask her what she meant exactly, or how she knew something was different. But those deeper conversations could come later. "Thank you. We will cherish this."

Around the room the others were quiet, some of them wiping at tears once more. "That's beautiful, Kendra." Ashley was the first of them to speak. "Erin would've loved knowing that."

Kendra smiled as she handed gifts to Ashley and her siblings. Each of them received a small heart-shaped stone with the same words engraved on it. *The Heart Remembers.* Then Kendra pulled one more gift from the bag. A smaller one. "This" — she looked across the room — "is for you, Amy."

And with that, the entire room fell silent. Everyone seemed to be holding their breath. And if John knew his kids and grandkids, they were doing something else, also.

Praying for Amy . . . and the moment ahead.

All night long, Amy couldn't take her eyes off the woman. Amy still wanted to be here, still wanted to meet Kendra. But she couldn't seem to find the words to talk to her. Every time she thought about going up and saying something, the timing didn't seem right.

Like they were eating dinner or praying in a circle or listening to Uncle Luke and Aunt Reagan and her cousins singing on the front porch. There wasn't really a chance for Amy to talk to the lady alone.

Until now.

Amy could feel everyone looking at her, but she didn't care. She stood and walked toward Kendra. "You brought me a Christmas present?"

"I did." Kendra got down on her knees and held out the little wrapped gift. "No one here misses your mommy more than you." Kendra's voice was quiet and sad and real. All at the same time. "I'm sorry about that, Amy. I meant what I said. If I could trade with your mom, I would. So she could be here with you."

Amy started to cry. Not because she was sad to spend more time with Kendra. But because Kendra understood exactly how she felt. She wanted her mommy to be here so badly. But since her mommy had to be with the rest of her family in heaven, it was very nice to know Kendra got to be alive.

And that her mommy had helped make that possible. Her mommy and God, of course.

Amy pressed her hands to her eyes and wiped away her tears. It wasn't nice to cry when someone just gave you a Christmas present. When she could see better, she opened the gift. Inside was a little velvet box. Amy opened that, too, and lying in the box was a gold heart necklace.

"It's a locket." Kendra helped Amy take the necklace from the box. "See?" The heart had a little door on it, and inside was a picture of her mother. She looked young and happy and pretty.

"My mommy . . ." Amy ran her thumb over the picture.

"Yes." Kendra was crying a little. "I have your mommy's heart, Amy. But you do, too. You always will. Because your mom is always with you." Kendra put her hand on Amy's shoulder. "I thought a heart necklace would help you remember that."

Amy looked from the necklace to Kendra. "How did you find her picture?"

Kendra looked at Amy's papa and then back at Amy. "I had a little help." She held up the necklace. "Can I put it on you?"

"Yes, please." Amy stood very still as Kendra unhooked the necklace and then fastened it around Amy's neck. Kendra smiled at her, even though her eyes were wet. "Do you like it?"

"It's perfect." Amy looked at the open heart, and the small picture of her mommy, and slowly she closed the locket and pressed it soft against her chest. "Thank you, Kendra.

"Can I . . . can I feel your heart?" She had been afraid to ask, afraid Kendra would say no. But she had to at least try.

Kendra looked like she wasn't sure. But then she did a little smile. "Of course." She took Amy's hand gently in her own and pressed it against her chest. And all of a sudden Amy could feel her mother's heartbeat. The way she had felt it when she was little and her mommy held her, or when she was scared at night and her mom would sit with her on the edge of her bed. Or when she'd sit on her mommy's lap and listen to a story.

Or when she'd cuddle with her mommy on Christmas morning.

Amy went to Kendra then and hugged her. For a long time. And as she did she could feel her mommy's heartbeat again. "Thank you."

"Of course, honey." Kendra held her again.

As Amy held on, she pretended just for a minute that her mommy was here. That she was safe in her arms and that she didn't have to miss her ever again. But then she blinked a few times and looked at Kendra. This wasn't her mother. Kendra was just a nice lady with her mommy's heart.

No, her mommy was never coming back. No one could take her place. But she knew her mommy was still alive because she was in heaven. And one day they would all be together again. Her whole family. Until then, her mommy had left a piece of herself behind to help Kendra live. But that wasn't all. She had left a piece of her heart *inside* Amy, too.

The heart around her neck would remind her of that.

Now and forever.

CHAPTER FOURTEEN

Dessert was being prepared in the kitchen, but Maddie wasn't hungry. She was too overwhelmed by all that had happened that night with Kendra and Amy. And so, while everyone else was eating, she found a quiet spot by the Christmas tree. The ornaments on Aunt Ashley's tree were nearly all photos, memories of Christmases past.

Until she came to Christmas Eve dinner, Maddie still hadn't felt quite right about God or her life, really. Yes, she was happy for Hayley. God had answered her prayer about a miracle for her sister, no question. No matter what happened with Patrick, she sensed God wanted her to know Hayley wouldn't be alone. She was happy and loving and capable of so much more than Maddie had imagined.

Despite what the drowning had taken.

Then there was the miracle of Uncle Luke and Aunt Reagan and their family getting here safely. Whatever had happened with the snowplow, there was no question God had given them a miracle. But even then Maddie still wondered about her own life.

Especially where Connor Flanigan was concerned.

She kept thinking about how she had pushed him away, and shut down all communication. So rude. He was probably glad to be done with her. No surprise he wasn't making an effort to see her now. He probably couldn't wait to get back to Liberty and spend time with people who cared about him.

Girls who would actually talk to him.

The whole situation with Connor had taken some of the shine off Christmas.

Right up until the moment they had just witnessed.

Maddie hadn't given much thought to the fact that the woman had her Aunt Erin's heart. Having someone's heart didn't mean that person took the place of the one who died. Not at all. Maddie's parents were both doctors — she knew a heart transplant was more of a medical procedure.

But when Kendra gave Amy the locket, when she told her that they each would forever have a part of Amy's mommy's heart . . . something lifted in Maddie's soul.

And all at once the shine of Christmas came back. In Amy's eyes, Maddie could see hope and healing again.

And if that wasn't a Christmas miracle, nothing was.

Peace settled over Maddie and she leaned her head against the back of the sofa. *God, you're so amazing. To let little Amy have a better understanding of her losses, a better picture of how her mother's life made a difference even in death. Meeting Kendra today was another miracle. One that Amy needed.*

And maybe all of us, too.

She stared at the tree, at a picture of the Baxter cousins long ago. Before the drowning. And suddenly a thought hit her. If Kendra had felt guilty about having the new heart, the gift would've been wasted. Aunt Erin wouldn't want the woman to go around feeling badly about what had happened.

And Hayley wouldn't want her to feel bad either.

Yes, she had the gift of a healthy life while Hayley had struggled ever since her accident. But Maddie's guilt didn't make things better for Hayley. It was like wasting the gift of life. And if Kendra wasn't going to waste her gift of a new heart, what right did Maddie have to punish herself by not living?

She took her phone from the pocket of her dark jeans. Whatever Connor was doing today, he hadn't been in touch. She wanted to text him and apologize again, tell him that the distance between them was all her fault. But she didn't want to appear desperate.

Besides, she didn't believe in chasing after a guy. That was a boy's job, to work hard to get a girl to like him. The problem was Connor had done that. But with every effort he made, Maddie had pushed him away.

She may have lost her chance with Connor, but she knew now she hadn't lost her chance with God. She lifted her eyes to the photo ornament of all the cousins again. *You're with us, God. I believe that now. You've made Your presence known in every situation this Christmas.*

And as for Connor . . . what happened was my own fault.

At least I learned from it.

That much was true. If she ever had the chance, she would share her story with Connor. And if not Connor, then she would share it with whomever God brought into her life. Friends or . . . someday . . . that special guy God had planned for her.

She was finished hiding her feelings. In fact, sometime in the next few days she would tell her parents everything, about the guilt she'd been carrying all these years.

Her way of thinking about Hayley had been wrong. God wouldn't want her to carry around guilt the rest of her life. She knew that now. And He wouldn't want her to push away His blessings out of some self-directed thought that she didn't deserve them.

Of course she didn't deserve God's blessings. None of them did. But that didn't give her the right to cut off His goodness, to push away the plans and people He brought into her life. God had good plans for Hayley. And He had good plans for her.

She called up Jeremiah 29:11 on her phone's Bible app. *For I know the plans I have for you, declares the Lord. Plans to prosper you and not to harm you, plans to give you hope and a future.* Maddie exhaled and again the peace of God surrounded her.

His plans might not be clear yet. But one day they would be. And she would never again reject happiness because of guilt over Hayley. Instead she would believe God's best for both of them. Because God was real. She knew that now.

As real as Christmas itself.

The Flanigan family dinner took longer

than usual. Bailey was not even three months pregnant, and still not feeling well. Which meant that Connor and his brothers took over much of the preparation and all of the cleaning.

Connor didn't mind.

Working in the kitchen took his thoughts off Maddie West. She had wanted to talk after the show the other night, but Connor had been busy ever since. Maybe after Christmas. Or maybe he wasn't as ready to talk with her now, anyway. If she could change so quickly, maybe Maddie West simply wasn't the girl for him.

Connor wasn't sure. He still thought about her all the time, but he was hesitant now. Either way, the day had been fun. Both sets of grandparents had joined them for Christmas Eve service and then prime rib dinner at the Flanigan house. Around the table they played the question game — one of Connor's favorites. Bailey's question had been the best.

If you could ask God one question, what would it be?

Some of his brothers' answers were funny — as always. Shawn said he'd ask God why the giraffe has such a long neck, and Justin would ask why animals had tails. But a few of them had really profound questions they

195

would ask God. BJ said he'd ask God why he and Justin and Shawn had the chance to be adopted into the Flanigan family when so many millions of kids never had that kind of opportunity.

Bailey said she'd ask God when exactly He had first dreamed up Brandon Paul for her. Which made everyone around the table smile.

Connor said he would ask God why they couldn't each have a window to their future. "So we would know for sure that everything works out. That we would find the right girl and have the right job. All those important details."

His question had been personal — especially in light of Maddie. Of course, he knew why God didn't allow such a thing. With the Lord, the journey was the destination. Every morning, every night, every step in between was a walk of faith. Otherwise there would be no need for a relationship with Jesus.

The dishes were just about finished, and already their grandparents had gone home for the night. Connor's mom came up beside him and grabbed a fresh towel. "I'll help dry. The Baxters are expecting us."

"We haven't been there in a while." Connor remembered visiting the Baxter family every year or so. Often his family had joined them for their annual Fourth of July picnic at Lake Monroe. But not for a few years.

"We haven't gotten together since the accident, the one that took Erin and Sam Hogan and three of their daughters."

Connor remembered the accident, and how the whole town of Bloomington had grieved the loss of the family. A truck driver had fallen asleep and rear-ended them. There were five white crosses at the side of the interstate where the accident happened. Connor drove by them each time he left town on his way back to Liberty University.

"Did they just not want a lot of friends over since then?" Connor washed the last casserole dish and handed it to his mother.

"I think it worked both ways. We wanted to give them space, a chance to be together as a family. Time to heal." She took the clean dish from Connor and dried it. "This Christmas they asked us to come for dessert and Pictionary. It takes time to be able to laugh again."

"I get that." Connor thought for a minute. "They have a bunch of kids, right?"

"Lots." His mom smiled. "They're not always all there. But I got a text from Ashley half an hour ago. Everyone's there tonight."

"That'll be fun." Connor dried his hands on the towel.

Connor's dad walked into the kitchen. "The boys and I got the trash out. Everyone ready?"

A smile lifted Connor's heart. He loved being home. Loved the everydayness of the Flanigan family together, how they helped each other. And tonight both families would make for a celebration they'd all remember.

Connor had no doubt.

CHAPTER FIFTEEN

They were about to serve dessert, and Kendra had only one disappointment. The night was flying by too fast. She was in the kitchen whipping a batch of fresh cream when she caught a glimpse of Amy in the next room, talking to Ashley.

The two had their heads together, as Amy showed off the photo of her mother in the locket. Kendra smiled to herself. The gift had been the perfect way to find a connection with the child. Holding her for those few seconds had awakened a longing in Kendra that hadn't been there since the surgery.

A longing for a child of her own.

Moe was still at the dining room table talking with John and Elaine, and now in the kitchen, some of the Baxter sisters were slicing pie and making coffee. Kendra felt more alive just being here, as if the presence of this family and their faith were air to her lungs.

Ashley came up and handed her a crystal bowl. "For the cream." She smiled. "Whenever you're done."

"That'll do it." Kendra turned off the beaters. The cream looked perfect. "Hey, Ashley. Thank you. For letting me and Moe come tonight."

"It all worked out. Your gift for Amy was very kind." Erin's sister leaned against the counter, the air between them much more relaxed than earlier when they first met.

"I had to find some way to connect with her."

"The locket was exactly what she needed." Ashley's voice was kind. "Proof that God wanted the two of you to meet."

"Maybe so." Kendra thought about Ashley's words, how easily she talked about God. As if He were right here in the room with them.

Ashley found a spoon for the cream. "So . . . you and Moe? My dad told me he wasn't going to come tonight."

"He wasn't. Not until yesterday." Kendra wasn't sure how much to say. "We . . . neither of us have ever believed in God."

Ashley listened. If she already knew this information, she didn't let on.

"Anyway . . . Moe and I, we weren't doing very well. Not since the transplant. We even talked about getting a divorce." She gave Ashley a wary look. "In the next month or so."

"Mmmm." Ashley looked genuinely troubled by this. "I'm sorry. Marriage is so important."

"Yes, it is." Kendra wasn't sure why she was telling Ashley this. They were strangers, after all. But somehow Kendra no longer felt that way. "Eventually I decided to challenge God — if there was a God. To see if He was real or just part of the imaginations of very nice people." She looked at Ashley. "Is that terrible?"

"Not at all." Ashley's smile held a knowing. "One day I'll have to tell you my story. How I went through a phase of not believing in God. I asked Him to show Himself, to prove He was real." Her quiet laugh seemed to suggest she was still amazed at what happened next. "Let's just say God has no trouble proving Himself."

"Right." Kendra dished the cream into the crystal bowl. "So I prayed for Moe. I asked God — if He was really there — to change Moe's attitude. So that our marriage would have a chance." She looked out at Moe still talking with John Baxter at the table. "Since then, we've been doing better than ever.

Which isn't even possible based on how things were just a few weeks ago." She looked at Ashley. "So if God is real — and it seems like He must be — I guess Moe and I have to decide what to do next."

Ashley smiled and nodded. "He'll show you that, too." She took the bowl of whipped cream. "Nice talking to you, Kendra. I mean it about telling you my story someday."

"I'd love to hear it."

As Ashley left to put the bowl with the other desserts, Moe found Kendra in the kitchen. He put his arms around her waist. "What an amazing night."

"I know." She looked straight into his eyes, at the warmth and kindness that hadn't been there before. "The Baxters are very special people."

"That's what I was going to tell you." He looked out into the room where the others were caught up in half a dozen conversations. "I can feel it, Kendra. The love here."

"It's in the air. A sort of love that fills my soul." She laid her head on his chest for a long moment. Then she looked at him again. "Don't you think, Moe . . . it could be something more?"

He searched her eyes. "Like God, you mean?"

"Maybe." She kissed him.

"And something else." His smile told her that he wasn't angry at her mentioning God. He was possibly even open to the idea. "Watching you with Amy . . ."

A soft gasp filled her throat. "You felt that, too?"

"Your doctor said you could have a baby, Kendra. Once everything was fine with your heart."

"That's exactly what I was thinking when Amy hugged me. I tried to imagine how I would feel having a little girl of my own. How special that would be."

For a long time Moe didn't say anything. He only looked into her eyes, straight through to her heart. Then he kissed her and smiled. "I think we have a lot to talk about when we get home." He paused. "Maybe we can join my sister at her church. Because . . . if God is real, it's about time we get to know Him."

"Really?"

Moe brushed his fingers against her cheek. "I love you, Kendra. I'm sorry . . . about everything."

"Me, too. I love you." She hadn't felt this much love for her husband since they were first married. "Merry Christmas."

"Merry Christmas."

From the other room, John called for

Moe. "Come tell Luke about that new tax law. He's a lawyer. The two of you probably speak the same language."

Moe smiled at Kendra. "We'll talk more later."

"Okay." She watched him go, watched him join the men at the table. Then she slipped into her coat and boots and stepped out onto the porch. The snow had let up and overhead the sky was clear. Stars dispelled the darkness, much as they must've that first Christmas night.

When Mary and Joseph welcomed the Savior of the world. The One who was God, in the flesh. The One still real and alive today. Kendra was suddenly sure about Him.

This night was all the proof she needed.

CHAPTER SIXTEEN

Maddie was still sitting by the tree, still talking to God and thanking Him for changing her heart, when the doorbell rang. She watched her Aunt Ashley hurry through the front room. "The Flanigans are here!"

The *Flanigans*? What? Maddie felt her eyes grow wide. The room seemed to tilt hard to one side. The *Flanigans*? In a rush of flashbacks, she remembered the name. The Flanigan family. Friends of her Aunt Ashley's. She hadn't seen them in years, but . . .

Was it possible?

Maddie stood, her back to the tree. It couldn't be possible. This family had young kids, and some of them were . . . some of them were adopted from Haiti.

Like Connor's brothers.

She held her breath as Aunt Ashley opened the door and welcomed the family inside. A blond boy was the first to enter. He introduced himself as Ricky. And then came three more boys — all of them teens. All of them black. Shawn, Justin, and BJ.

Her knees trembled. Next through the door came . . .

"Bailey!" Maddie took a few steps forward. "Bailey Paul? You're . . . you're part of the Flanigan family? My Aunt Ashley's friends? I was so young back then . . . And I guess my family missed a lot of those parties. I can't believe this."

"Maddie West?" Bailey hurried over to her. "This is crazy! I had no idea you were part of the Baxter family! I haven't been to Ashley Baxter's house in years."

"Makes sense." Maddie laughed. "There's a ton of us Baxter grandkids."

The two hugged and just then Brandon, Bailey's parents, and finally Connor entered the house.

He saw her and immediately froze. For what seemed like ten minutes, Maddie felt as if they were the only ones in the room. He was carrying another dessert, and slowly he set it on a nearby end table. "Maddie?"

"I can't believe this."

Their parents and families were oblivious to what was happening between them. Only Bailey and Brandon stood by, grinning at what they were witnessing. Maddie heard

206

Bailey say something about none of them knowing she was part of the Baxter family.

But Maddie couldn't concentrate on anything or anyone but Connor.

He crossed the room to her. "I . . . can't believe you're here." He hugged her and took a step back. "No wonder you looked familiar."

"How come I didn't figure this out?" She still felt dizzy, as if she couldn't quite get the details to add up. "I forgot my aunt's friends were the Flanigans. Until just now as she was answering the door."

They hugged again and at that point Connor's parents joined them by the tree. Connor's cheeks were red, as if he, too, couldn't believe what had just happened. "Mom . . . Dad . . . this is Maddie West."

His mom smiled. "We've known Maddie since she was a little girl."

"Maddie and her sister, Hayley." Connor's dad grinned. "It's been a few years."

"At least a few." Maddie laughed. And for the next several minutes they worked to figure out the last time they were all together. Three years ago at the annual Fourth of July picnic, Connor had been on a camping trip with his church's high school group. And the year before that, Maddie had stayed home sick with her dad.

"So the last time we were both at one of these parties was six years ago." Connor looked at Maddie. "You were twelve and I was thirteen."

"I had braces." Maddie giggled.

"Me, too." Connor squinted at her, as if he were looking back through the years. "Was your hair dark back then?"

"Darker, for sure." She was still laughing. "I highlight it."

"It all makes sense now." Connor hugged her again, and this time he whispered near her face, "Let's talk later."

"Definitely," she whispered back.

They joined the others headed to the dining room, and after introductions everyone gathered at the two tables and ate dessert. The Flanigans shared about their question game and everyone took a turn answering the one Cole thought up.

"If you could have one gift that couldn't be wrapped, what would it be?"

Kendra Bryant went last. Her answer brought tears to almost everyone's eyes. "I'd have Erin and the rest of her family here with us." She looked around the room. "Because I think we would've been friends."

The time was poignant and beautiful, a perfect ending to a perfect Christmas Eve. And later, when people started to pack up

208

their things and leave, Maddie asked her mom and dad if they could stay a little longer. So she and Connor could have a few minutes together.

"Looks like you and I need to talk, too." Her mom brushed her knuckles against Maddie's cheek. "Wouldn't you say?"

"Yes." Maddie hugged her. "I have a lot to tell you."

"I'll look forward to it." Her mom smiled. "Take your time, honey."

"Thanks." Maddie returned the smile and then found Connor hanging out with her boy cousins. All of them seemed to remember him. Maybe that was part of the reason Maddie hadn't recognized him. He had probably hung out with her boy cousins whenever they were all together. She would've been with the girls. When she was twelve, the last thing she was thinking about was boys.

"You have a few minutes?" She grinned at him, and immediately he was on his feet.

"We'll plan that fishing trip later." He grinned at the guys. "Gotta run."

"Wait." Cole stood and looked from Maddie back to Connor. "You two know each other?"

"We worked the Christmas play together." Maddie shot Cole a look that said he'd better not make any funny comments. "We need to catch up."

Cole nodded slowly. "Got it." He winked at Connor and then turned to the other boys. "I say we plan the fishing trip in March. As soon as the snow starts to melt. That's when trout bite the best."

They were still talking about fishing as Maddie and Connor walked into the next room, with the Christmas tree. They were the only ones there, and Maddie was thankful. She still couldn't believe that Connor was here, and that the conversation she'd been wanting was finally going to happen. Here.

On Christmas Eve.

They sat next to each other in the dark, with just the glow of the tree to light the moment. "I didn't think we'd have time for this till next week." Connor turned so he could see her better. "I never would've dreamed you were part of the Baxter family. I forget that most of you have different last names."

"And you . . . I should've put the pieces together. But Bailey and I were too many years apart when we were younger. She was either off with one of her friends or hanging out with your mom. Anyway, I don't think of her as from around here. Because of

Brandon, I guess."

For a few seconds Connor only looked at her. "So . . . about you and me." He allowed a soft laugh and his eyes found the tree. "It seemed like we were great, like we had something special. And then you pulled away."

"I know . . ." Maddie wanted to get to the truth as quickly as possible. "It was all my fault."

"Maybe it was mine. I kept thinking, I must've said something that offended you. Or maybe there was something about the way I acted that you didn't like." He looked at her, the tree lights reflecting in his eyes. "I just couldn't think what it was."

"No. That wasn't it." Her voice was quiet, meant for him alone. In the next room they could hear the others laughing and sharing stories. But here it was just the two of them. Exactly how Maddie wanted it. "I was keeping the truth from you, Connor. I had to. But now . . . now I know I was wrong to do that."

"The truth?"

"Yes." She sighed. *God, help me find a way to tell him everything. I want to be honest.* A new sense of strength filled her heart. Maddie took a deep breath. "Do you remember I told you that my sister had health issues?"

"Yes." Connor narrowed his eyes, as if he were seeing back through the years. "Was she . . . did she drown? When she was really little? Was that your sister?"

"It was." The pain of what had happened never dimmed. Maddie was sure it never would. "She was three and I was five. I was supposed to be watching her."

"At your house?" Connor searched her eyes. "Maddie, that could never be your fault."

"We were at a birthday party. My dad was there because my mom was on call at the hospital that day." She could see it all again, smell the flowers on the birthday table and the sugary sweet of the icing on the chocolate cake.

"They had a pool?" Connor was completely engaged, listening to every word.

"Yes." She felt sick to her stomach recounting the story, but she had to. She'd stuffed the details to the bottom of her heart for too many years. "It was a swim party. Everyone had life jackets, but then it was time to eat cake and we all took them off. Hayley was the youngest there. And my dad . . . he told me to watch her. To make sure she didn't go near the pool with her life jacket off."

Connor groaned, as if the story was causing him physical pain. "Maddie . . ."

"And then . . ." Tears stung her eyes, but she refused to give in to them. ". . . I remember Hayley running past me, heading out back with a few other kids. And . . . she didn't have her life jacket on." Maddie hung her head. Two tears slid down her cheeks.

"Hey . . . it's okay. You were little, Maddie." Connor took hold of her hand.

"I yelled at her, 'Get your life jacket, Hayley. You have to wear it.' " Maddie shook her head, trapped in that day all over again. "She didn't stop, didn't answer me. And then . . . she was gone out back." Maddie lifted her eyes to Connor. "I could've stopped her, but . . . I didn't. I just . . . let her go."

Connor didn't say anything. He ran his thumb slowly over her hand and listened.

"A little while later I knew something was wrong. Hayley wasn't anywhere. She was just . . . she was gone. And I started calling her name. Over and over again."

"What about your dad?"

"He was up right away, calling for her, too. Shouting her name. Then everyone was calling for her."

Without saying a word, Connor reached out and put his hand alongside her face.

The gesture was enough to melt Maddie's

heart. It was the last thing she'd expected him to do. Show her grace and understanding. All her life she thought that if she was honest about Hayley, people would turn and run.

But not Connor.

She blinked and a few tears ran down her cheeks. "Sorry. Every day I think about what happened to Hayley. How I could've stopped her. I watched her go outside. Without her life jacket. So it was my fault. But I've never . . . told anyone."

"You were too little, Maddie. You couldn't have known what would happen." Connor ran his thumb along the side of her hand again. "I'm here, Maddie. It's okay."

"Anyway . . ." She stared at the tree, at the ornament of all the cousins together. "We ran out back and she was there . . . at the bottom of the pool. She . . . wasn't moving."

Connor gave her hand the most gentle squeeze. "I wish you hadn't had to see that."

"I wish it hadn't happened." She took a quick breath and finished the story. "My dad dove in right away and brought her to the top."

"She was breathing?" Connor's voice was quiet.

"Not at first. The doctors didn't get her

breathing until she was at the hospital. I guess they told my parents she'd never walk or talk. That she'd be blind the rest of her life." She paused. "I didn't know that until recently."

Connor looked surprised. "They were wrong, obviously."

"Yes." Maddie was beyond thankful for the ways God had answered their prayers. "But she's still not . . . the same. You know?"

Maddie realized that Connor hadn't been around Hayley enough to notice. But even so he nodded. "Yeah. She sat across from us during dessert. I could tell something was different. But it's nothing really major, Maddie. At least it didn't seem like it tonight."

"She's still improving. That's another miracle." Maddie felt the sadness in her smile. "So . . . that's the part I never told you."

Connor was still holding her hand, and now he looked long into her eyes. "I hate that you had to go through that. When you were so little." She had never seen anyone look at her with such compassion. "But why . . . why did that make you pull away from me these last few weeks?"

This was the hardest part, the part she wasn't sure he'd understand. She exhaled, searching for the right words. "I've always known it was my fault. What happened to Hayley. Sure, I was little. And maybe it was too much responsibility for someone my age." Her voice broke. "But still, it was my fault. So if Hayley could never have a normal life, then I didn't deserve one either."

Confusion clouded Connor's eyes. "A normal life?"

"Like . . . if Hayley could never fall in love" — Maddie's voice fell to little more than a whisper — "I couldn't either."

Suddenly what she was saying must've become clear to Connor. The look on his face shifted and she could see just how much he cared. How much he liked her. "So you pulled away from me."

"Yes." She looked at him, all the way through to his soul. "Does that make sense?"

Connor looked deep into her eyes. "First . . . you were five years old, Maddie. What happened to Hayley wasn't your fault."

"I can still hear my dad telling me to watch her. 'Maddie, keep an eye on your little sister . . . Don't take your eyes off her.' " She looked down for several seconds before lifting her gaze back to his. "I

216

watched her go outside, Connor. I watched her and I didn't stop her." She sighed. It felt better to finally tell the truth about what happened. Even if it didn't change things.

"You have to let it go. You didn't know what would happen."

"I guess." Her heart felt free, even though the weight of her actions remained. "I know God doesn't want me to feel guilty anymore. But still . . . it was my fault."

"You were five." Connor didn't break eye contact, not even for a moment. "Maddie, can you tell me something? Did you blame your father for what happened?"

"No." She was quick to answer. "Not at all. It was my job to look after her."

"He was the adult. He was the one in charge." Connor's tone was full of kindness and understanding. "I'm sure he blames himself every day. The same way you've been doing. Your mother, too. She was at work instead of spending the afternoon with you and Hayley at the party."

Connor's words made sense. They were a balm that soothed the pain Maddie had carried since that awful day so many years ago. He wasn't finished. "What about the person who owned the home? Or the girl having the birthday party? They could blame themselves, too. If only one of the moms had been out back watching the pool. Or if they would've had a different sort of birthday party — maybe one at the park or at a pizza place."

Maddie couldn't imagine blaming any of them. "It wasn't their fault."

"But I bet there are times when they all wonder. Don't you think?"

The possibility filled Maddie's heart and hurt her at the same time. "I guess . . . I never imagined that. Up until now, I've always seen what happened through *my* eyes. My guilt over it."

"And you know what the truth is?" Connor didn't waver, didn't hesitate. "The truth is, accidents happen." He pulled out his phone and opened his Bible app. "I was reading John 16 in my devotions today."

Maddie felt herself falling for him. What college guy actually had devotion time with God?

He pulled up a section of Scripture. "Here, in verse thirty-three. It says, *'In this world you will have trouble. But be of good cheer, for I have overcome the world.'* " He put his phone down and clicked it off. "See, Maddie? Bad things happen. Period."

She nodded. She was so choked up over his kindness that she couldn't think of anything to say.

"It wasn't your fault or anyone else's fault. That's not where God wants you to put your focus."

"Meaning what?"

Connor allowed the hint of a smile. "He wants you to focus on Him. How He got your family through that time. How He healed Hayley . . . how He's still healing her."

The idea felt so freeing, Maddie couldn't stop the tears. She squeezed her eyes shut and covered her face with her hands. All this time . . . every day since Hayley's accident, she had refused to let herself feel too good or too happy or too caught up in a boy like Connor Flanigan.

All because she had blamed herself.

But now . . . maybe Connor was right. Maybe she wasn't the only one who had been feeling guilty about Hayley. And if that was true, maybe all of them were wrong to carry the blame. Especially when God had worked a miracle to heal her, to give her sight and speech and the ability to attend school. Hayley was walking proof of God's love and faithfulness.

Before this Maddie had chosen only to see her sister's broken parts. The missing parts. But not anymore.

"Hey . . ." He crooked his finger and lifted

219

her chin so their eyes met. "I only wish you would've told me back at the beginning."

A smile started in her heart and made its way to her face. "Wanna hear something amazing?"

"Yes." He leaned against the arm of the sofa, his eyes deep. "Always."

"At the Christmas play, Hayley brought a friend. A boy." She grinned, feeling all over again the happiness she'd felt for her sister that night. "His name is Patrick. He has some special needs, but he's highly functional. Same as her."

Connor smiled, the mood lighter between them. "So she's getting ahead of you. Is that what you're saying?"

Laughter tickled Maddie's throat. "I guess. But I promised myself I was finished comparing her life to mine. God has good plans for both of us." She felt her eyes light up. "Remember the Christmas miracle I was praying for?"

"*We* were praying for." His look was more flirty and fun. The heaviness gone.

"Yes, that's right. You were praying, too." She loved how he made her feel. How could she have pulled away from him? "Well, Patrick was the miracle. If Hayley can have love one day, then I know God is here and He's real."

"And tonight . . . your uncle Luke and aunt Reagan's story about being stuck in the snow?"

"Yes, another one." She softened her voice again. "And you should've seen my cousin Amy meeting Kendra Bryant, the woman who has her mother's heart."

"What?" Connor looked amazed. "That's definitely another story."

"Yes. And another miracle."

Connor met her eyes again and it felt like the two of them were the only ones in the house. "And this, Maddie . . . seeing you here." His eyes shone again, as if there was more he wanted to say. Words that would have to wait for the right time.

Maddie was so happy she could barely breathe. Watching Connor walk through the door, she knew the two of them having this time together was another gift from God. Because not only did it clear up things with Connor. It had allowed her heart to be free and light and whole again.

For the first time since she was five.

CHAPTER SEVENTEEN

It was a Christmas Eve John would remember for the rest of his life. And now it was time for Kendra and Moe to leave. John and Elaine walked them to the foyer, the conversation easy as they made their way. Already Dayne and Katy and Kari and Ryan had taken their children home. Ashley had put Janessa and Amy to bed, and the others were wrapping things up.

When they reached the front door, Kendra turned to John. "Tonight meant more to me than you'll ever know." She linked arms with Moe. "The two of us . . . we talked about it a few minutes ago. We're going to church tomorrow with Moe's sister."

Moe nodded. "I can't say I believe in God. Not yet, anyway. But I can take this step." He looked at Kendra. "We can take it together."

And in that moment, Christmas came over John in a way he had never quite felt before.

"That's amazing." He smiled at the couple. "First steps. I like that."

Elaine put her arm around John's waist. "There's no time like Christmas to examine your beliefs. It's one of the main reasons John reached out to you. So we could share our faith."

"Not just our faith. But Erin's faith. Her family's faith." John smiled at Elaine and then at Kendra. He paused for a long while. "But I also knew I wanted to be in the same room again with Erin's beating heart. She was my little girl. The last time I hugged her, I didn't know . . . I'd never have another chance to hold her again.

"It'll be a journey. Just remember that. Believing God truly is just the first step." John put his hand on Moe's shoulder. "We're here for you. If you want to meet again."

"Good to know. Oh . . . and also . . . we talked about something else." Moe smiled at Kendra.

"Yes." Kendra turned to John. "After tonight . . . we'd like to have a baby. Being around all your grandkids, Moe and I were both thinking about that."

It was another victory, another reason John was sure this was how they were supposed to celebrate Christmas Eve after all.

He still couldn't believe that even Luke and Ashley and their families had joined them tonight. But he was grateful.

He and Elaine hugged Kendra and Moe again, wishing them a merry Christmas, and thanking them for coming. This had indeed been the right decision. For Kendra, for Amy, for the whole family. And as Kendra and Moe drove away, John smiled. Because after tonight they would no longer be strangers.

But family.

They had joined the others for Pictionary, and now everyone was finding coats and saying their goodbyes. Connor didn't want to leave Maddie yet, but he had a feeling they'd see each other often in the next few days.

He pulled her aside as their families were making their way to the front door. "This has been the most . . . amazing Christmas Eve." He stood with her in the doorway to the living room, where they'd spent so much time talking earlier. "I mean . . . it was basically a reunion."

"Right." She laughed. Her eyes looked years lighter than they had before their talk. "Last time we were together here, we probably played hide-and-seek in the garden out back."

"Yes." He nodded, his tone teasing. "I think I remember that. I was four and you were three."

"It's possible."

"True." He took a step closer to her. "After tonight, anything's possible." Connor wasn't sure how things might go from here. But if he had it his way, Maddie would be his girlfriend before Valentine's Day. It was a possibility he would talk about with his parents, and hers.

An idea he would pray about.

Suddenly something overhead caught his eye. He looked up, and sure enough. Mistletoe hung from the doorframe. Everyone else was out front, and Maddie only had a minute before she had to leave.

She followed his gaze and her cheeks grew a pretty shade of pink. "Mistletoe."

"Yep." Connor took hold of both her hands. He shrugged. "It's sort of a tradition."

"True." She didn't blink, didn't look away.

Connor leaned in and for the most wonderful, brief moment, he kissed her. Her lips were soft and warm against his and her nearness filled his senses. It was a kiss Connor was sure he'd remember forever. He eased back, a little breathless. "This needs to be our tradition." He smiled at her, searching her eyes. "Right here. Under the mistletoe. Every Christmas."

"Every Christmas?" Her eyes sparkled and her laughter told him she had enjoyed the moment as much as him.

He grinned. "Every single one."

They walked to the front door and he helped her with her coat. As she left he hugged her. "Merry Christmas, Maddie."

"Merry Christmas."

Connor had a single thought as he watched her walk into the snowy night with her parents and her sister. He didn't need to wonder what gift he would want that couldn't be wrapped.

Her name was Maddie West.

And because of her, after tonight, he would never be the same again.

CHAPTER EIGHTEEN

The house was quiet, everyone asleep except Ashley and Landon. She found him near the Christmas tree, hands in his pockets, staring at the ornaments. "I love our tree."

"I loved tonight." She took her spot beside him, and he put his arm around her shoulders. "I can't imagine if we would've missed it."

"Kendra was wonderful. She fit in so easily." Landon looked at Ashley, his eyes soft. "I kept forgetting she wasn't someone we'd known for years."

"Me, too. And what she said about Erin . . . I'll remember that always."

Landon sighed. "We still have some work to do, you and me."

Ashley laughed. "True. It is Christmas Eve. The kids will be up bright and early."

Their tradition was the same every year. They wrapped presents for the kids and hid them in their closet. Then late on Christmas Eve when everyone else was asleep they set them out in piles — one for each of the children. The final touch was always the kids' stockings — embroidered with their names.

"Thank you." Ashley turned to her husband. "Thanks for putting up with me."

"Ash . . . I've loved you as far back as I can remember."

"I know." She framed his face with her hands. "But sometimes I'm not the easiest. Like the whole avoidance plan. I was wrong, but you never said so. You let me figure things out on my own."

"I understand you. That's all." He ran his fingers through her hair. "You feel so much, Ash. I love that about you."

"And I feel most for you." She studied his eyes, his handsome face. "You were praying for me, weren't you? That I'd change my mind and join the others tonight."

"Hmmm." He grinned. "Maybe."

"I knew it." She laughed and kissed him. "I love you so much."

"I love you, too. I always have." Landon returned the kiss.

For a long moment they forgot about the Christmas presents and the stockings. But then they heard a sound behind them. Ashley turned around first.

There, standing in the doorway in her red flannel Christmas nightgown was Amy. She was still wearing her heart locket.

"Hi." Her voice was soft.

"Honey, we thought you were asleep." Ashley went to her and hugged her shoulders. "Is everything okay?"

"Yes, sorry." Amy looked up at her. "It's just . . . I couldn't sleep." She fiddled with the heart locket and stared at the picture inside. Then she lifted her eyes to Ashley again. "I wanted to thank you. For letting me meet Kendra."

"Aww, honey . . . of course. As soon as I knew that's what you wanted, me and Uncle Landon changed our minds right away."

"I know." Amy smiled. "That's why I wanted to thank you." She closed the locket and held her free arm out to Landon. "Can you come here, too?"

Landon did as she asked. "We're so glad you got to meet her, sweetie."

Amy hugged them both and after several seconds she looked first to Ashley and then to Landon. "I loved meeting Kendra, and I loved hearing my mommy's heartbeat again. But I wanted you to know something."

"Okay, honey. We're listening." Ashley felt beyond touched. Whatever Amy was about to say, it clearly was important.

"Kendra will never be my family. She's a nice lady and she's right. Me and her both have a piece of my mommy's heart. That'll always be true." Amy hugged Ashley again and then Landon. "But you two . . . you're my family. And that's the greatest Christmas gift of all."

Ashley and Landon both knelt down near Amy and held her close. "That's the most beautiful thing you could say." Ashley kissed the girl's cheek. "We feel the same way."

"That's right." Landon smoothed Amy's hair and smiled at her. "You're our family, too. You always will be."

After that, Amy seemed more relaxed. She yawned and fiddled with her heart locket again. "It's probably a good idea if I go to bed now."

"Yes." Ashley stood and Landon did the same. "Goodnight, Amy. We love you."

She smiled. "Love you, too. For always."

After that, Amy padded up the stairs to bed. As soon as she was out of sight, Landon pulled Ashley into his arms. "Wow. That was amazing."

"You're amazing." Ashley held on to him. If she could freeze this night she would. Each of their kids healthy and happy and ready to share a Christmas Day together.

And Landon — the man who years ago had loved her enough to take Cole as his own, the man who loved Amy enough to do the same thing all over again. "I'm who I am because of you, Landon." She brushed her face against his. "No one loves like you do."

"You make it easy, Ashley." Landon kissed her, and then he took her by the hand back to their bedroom closet. If this was like other Christmas Eves, they were still an hour from climbing into bed. Enough time to put out the gifts and talk about Christmases gone by. Time to think back on the year past and dream about the one ahead. And time to remember the greatest gift God had given them.

The one that couldn't be wrapped.

The gift of family.

Dear Reader Friend,

Being back with the Baxter family has been the greatest Christmas gift I could've asked for. Always when people ask me, "How are the Baxters?" I have an answer. I honestly do. I can see them at work and play, holding close conversations, and looking for new horizons. Participating in never-seen-before adventures.

Yes, it's a pleasure to be back with the Baxter family.

And so I've decided to write more Baxter books. These stories will give you a window to the grown Baxter kids and their families, their faith walks, career challenges, and the life-changing difference they are making in the world around them.

You've probably heard by now that the Baxter family is coming to TV. The series is expected to become one of the most beloved of all time. I know you'll be watching. But I also know you'll be reading.

Because the Baxter family isn't just my family. It's your family.

And with them at the middle of our lives, we are all family.

Until next time . . . thanks for being part of the story.

Love you!
Karen

THE QUESTION GAME

The Baxter family loves to play the Question Game around the dinner table. Especially during the holidays. The Question Game is simple. Someone comes up with a question, then everyone at the table takes a turn answering it. Sometimes great questions are a little difficult to come up with. So here are a few questions the Baxters have used over the years:

1. What gift that cannot be wrapped would you want most of all?
2. If you could ask God one question, what would it be?
3. If you could have one superpower, what would it be and why?
4. If you could be a professional athlete in any sport, what would it be?
5. You can have dinner with one family member who has passed on. Who would it be, and what would

you talk about?

6. You can have dinner with any of the twelve apostles. Who would you choose and what would you ask him?

7. You can have coffee with any person from American history. Who would you choose and why?

8. What was your favorite family vacation and why?

9. What are three of your favorite memories from Christmases gone by?

10. What was one of the best Christmas presents you ever received?

11. What was one of the best Christmas presents you ever gave?

12. What's your favorite Bible verse and why?

13. Who is your favorite Bible character and why?

14. What's your earliest childhood memory?

15. If you had a million dollars to spend on something — and you couldn't give it away — how would you use it?

16. What's one country you'd love to visit?

17. How would you handle fame and

what would you be famous for?

18. What three life lessons have mattered most to you?

19. What do you want people to remember you for?

20. If you could do anything for someone else, what would you do and for whom?

BAXTER FAMILY
THANKSGIVING DINNER

Many of you have asked over the years about the Baxter family Thanksgiving, what dishes they ate, and even how you might get the recipes for those dishes. And so . . . since this is a Christmas book . . . I thought I'd put together a menu for you. This is the Baxter Family Thanksgiving Menu:

Ashley's Stuffed Golden Turkey
Landon's Mashed Potatoes
Elizabeth's Sliced Sweet Potatoes
Baxter Christmas Salad
Cole's Corn Bread and Herb Stuffing
Organic Gravy
Baby Buttered Peas
Kari's Cheesy Biscuits
Black Olives
Dill Pickle Slices
*John's Baked Apple Crumble and Organic
Sweet Cream*

BAXTER FAMILY
THANKSGIVING TIMETABLE

Tuesday Before Thanksgiving

✳ Go grocery shopping. If buying a fresh turkey, this is the time to do it. If buying a frozen turkey, you'll want to have that in the refrigerator no later than Monday before Thanksgiving.

Wednesday Before Thanksgiving

✳ Make stuffing, store in gallon-size Ziploc bag in the refrigerator.
✳ Make Christmas Salad, cover and refrigerate.
✳ Make Sliced Sweet Potatoes, cover and put in the refrigerator. *Do not bake* until Thursday.
✳ Peel and slice apples for Baked Apple Crumble. Cover and refrigerate. *Do not bake* until Thursday.
✳ Make Cheesy Biscuits.

241

Thanksgiving Thursday

❊ Figure out what time to start working on the turkey.

❊ Stuff the turkey. Place leftover stuffing in a baking casserole dish.

❊ Place Sliced Sweet Potatoes in oven or Crock-Pot depending on oven space.

❊ Peel potatoes, boil.

❊ Place peas in a pot of water.

❊ Make the gravy. Set aside.

❊ Place cool biscuits on a cooking sheet to heat up after turkey comes out of oven.

❊ Drain water from potatoes, prepare according to recipe.

❊ Boil peas. Add butter and salt. Turn off heat and let sit in boiling water.

❊ After turkey comes out, remove some of the juices and add to the gravy.

❊ Warm biscuits.

❊ Place Baked Apple Crumble in oven to bake during dinner.

❊ Get the rest of the family to help place items in special dishes.

❊ Pray, thank God . . . and enjoy.

BAXTER FAMILY THANKSGIVING RECIPES

Ashley's Stuffed Golden Turkey

At the Baxter family Thanksgiving, Ashley is in charge of choosing the turkey these days. She goes through the following steps to find just the right turkey to grace the table for the holiday.

❋ Ashley chooses an organic turkey, free from antibiotics and hormones. Fresh or frozen doesn't matter. But if the turkey is frozen, Ashley sets a reminder for herself to move it from the freezer to the fridge so it can thaw. Calculate how long it will take to thaw your particular turkey.

❋ Use a baking bag to cut down on oven time and to keep the turkey tender and juicy.

❋ Do the math. Ashley likes to eat at 3:00 P.M., like the rest of the Baxter family.

Be sure to preheat the oven. So she calculates how long she'll need to cook a stuffed turkey. Then she allows 30 minutes to prep the turkey before baking and an additional 30 minutes for the turkey to set after removing it from the bag and carving. Ideally, she takes the turkey out of the oven 40 minutes before dinner is served.

❋ Based on your calculations, choose the exact time to begin working on the turkey on Thanksgiving morning. Then take the turkey out of the fridge, remove the wrapper and set the bird in a clean sink. Next remove the bag of giblets and the neck from the backside and front of the turkey.

❋ Once both cavities are clear, rinse with fresh, cool water, drain the water from the bird and set it in a pan. Ashley likes the disposable pans with metal handles and metal reinforcements that run on the bottom.

❋ Next, stuff the turkey with the dressing made the night before. Allow the stuffing to spill out of the bird so that it creates a nice rounded top to the stuffed area.

❋ Ashley likes to melt a stick of butter and rub it all over the outside of the turkey, including the rounded stuffing. Sprinkle with salt.

❄ Landon always helps Ashley with this next part. Take the baking bag and sprinkle a tablespoon of flour inside. Shake to cover the inside of the bag. Lift the turkey into the bag and twist the end of the bag. Set back inside the pan. Make a few 1-inch slits in the top of the bag. Place in oven.

LANDON'S MASHED POTATOES
The Baxter family likes to make lots of mashed potatoes. Even if they don't eat them all on Thanksgiving Day, they will definitely eat them as part of the leftovers throughout the weekend. Since the Baxters have so many family members, they sometimes go through 15 pounds of potatoes. Landon always takes on this job. It's gotten so that the Baxters look forward to the way Landon makes them. His special touch is one more reason they love Thanksgiving. Landon figures 1/3 to 1/2 pound per person. To make mashed potatoes the way the Baxter family does, follow these instructions:

❄ Peel potatoes, chop into 1/2-cup-size chunks, place in pot of cold water. Make sure potato pieces are covered by at least an inch of water.

❊ Boil until potatoes are soft enough for a fork to easily pass through. Stop before potatoes start to fall apart.

❊ Drain water. Then mash the cooked potatoes in their pan. Mash until all chunks are broken up. This will prevent lumps.

❊ Add 1 cup of milk for every 5 pounds of potatoes. Ashley sometimes uses half-and-half to make the potatoes more creamy.

❊ Add 1 stick of butter for every 5 pounds of potatoes.

❊ Add 1 teaspoon of salt for every 5 pounds of potatoes.

❊ Use beaters to lightly blend the ingredients.

❊ Add additional milk/cream, butter or salt to taste.

ELIZABETH'S SLICED SWEET POTATOES

This is one of the Baxter family's favorite dishes, and it's been around since the Baxter kids were little. Elizabeth made up the recipe herself when Luke was just a baby, and it was an instant hit that Thanksgiving. There was a time when Elizabeth added brown sugar to this recipe. But it's optional here. The Baxters have found that this dish is very sweet on its own, without any added sugar at all. Here is the recipe they follow:

* ❋ Peel sweet potatoes (buy 1 sweet potato for every 2 guests).
* ❋ Thinly slice the sweet potatoes (approximately 1/4-inch thick) and place slices in a large container.
* ❋ Melt 1 stick of butter for every 6-8 sweet potatoes. Pour the melted butter over the slices.
* ❋ Use large spoons to toss the butter evenly over the slices. Elizabeth found this to be the easiest way to coat the slices.
* ❋ Add 1 teaspoon salt for every 8 sweet potatoes. Sprinkle over the buttered slices and use spoons to spread evenly.
* ❋ Top with a sprinkle of cinnamon (optional — the Baxters don't do this every year).
* ❋ Place buttered, salted slices into a baking dish or Crock-Pot. Cover with tinfoil.
* ❋ Bake for 4 hours at 350 degrees. Remove tinfoil for the last 45 minutes.

BAXTER CHRISTMAS SALAD

Over the years, the Baxter family has loved this seasonal Jell-O salad. The little Baxter kids call it "the red stuff," but the right name is the Baxter Christmas Salad. Here's how to make this family favorite:

❄ Finely grind 1 bag of thin salted pretzel sticks. The Baxters use a food processor to accomplish this. Try to leave some 1/4-inch pieces in the mix.

❄ Place ground pretzels in a large bowl. Add 1 stick melted butter and 1/4 cup honey. Stir. The mixture should be moist enough to hold its shape. If not, add another 1/2 stick butter.

❄ Press into the bottom of a greased 13-by-9-inch glass casserole dish. It should be 1/2-inch deep, give or take.

❄ Bake for 20 minutes at 325 degrees.

❄ Take crust from the oven and let it cool.

❄ In a separate bowl beat 1 pint of heavy cream till it makes light peaks. Add 1 teaspoon vanilla and 2 tablespoons stevia confectioners' sugar.

❄ In another bowl mash 2 (8-ounce) bricks of cream cheese. Blend the whipped cream in and beat only until smooth. Add 1/4 cup Swerve confectioners' sugar. Blend only until mixed.

* Using a spatula, smooth the whipped cream/cream cheese mixture over the cooled pretzel crust. This layer should be about an inch thick.
* In yet another bowl, empty 1 packet regular or sugar-free strawberry Jell-O. Add 2 cups boiling water and stir until dissolved. Then add 1 cup cold water. Then add 1 bag sliced frozen strawberries.
* Immediately spoon the Jell-O mixture over the whipped cream/cream cheese layer. Cover with plastic wrap. Place in refrigerator to solidify. Serve cold from fridge.

COLE'S CORN BREAD AND HERB STUFFING

The Baxters used to make this stuffing with homemade bread crumbs. But now they've found an easier way. They buy bags of dry seasoned corn bread crumbs and bags of dry herb-seasoned bread crumbs. Instead of making one kind or the other, the Baxter family uses half of each type so that the stuffing is a mix of the two kinds. This is because when Cole was four years old, he mixed the two types on his plate and told everyone it was better that way. The next year, Ashley mixed the two on purpose —

and the family loved it. Then they like to add butter, broth, sautéed onions and sautéed celery. It's Cole's favorite!

ORGANIC GRAVY

The Baxters enjoy using an organic mix for their gravy base. Usually these mixes require 1 packet to each cup of water. This can be prepared ahead of time. Then make the gravy extra tasty by adding juice and fat from the cooked turkey. Just enough for flavor.

BABY BUTTERED PEAS

There are two types of frozen green peas — one large, and one very small. The smaller peas are generally more tender and sweeter. These are the frozen green peas the Baxters look for each Thanksgiving. Simply cover the frozen peas in a pan of water. Add 1/2 stick of butter and 1 teaspoon of salt per bag. Bring to a boil. Serve hot, using a spoon with holes.

KARI'S CHEESY BISCUITS

There was a time when the Baxter family would eat Hawaiian rolls with their Thanksgiving dinner. But several years ago Kari created a recipe that would give them a much healthier dinner roll. She tweaked a few recipes to come up with this:

1/2 cup coconut flour
1/2 cup almond flour
2 teaspoons baking powder
1/2 teaspoon salt
1 teaspoon garlic powder
1 cup mixed grated Colby Jack cheddar cheese
4 large eggs
1 cup sour cream
1/3 cup melted butter

* Preheat oven to 350 degrees.
* Mix all dry ingredients together.
* Add half the cheese.
* Mix in eggs, sour cream and melted butter.
* Add half the remaining cheese.
* Drop by spoonfuls onto a parchment-covered baking sheet.
* Sprinkle remaining cheese over biscuits.
* Bake 20 minutes, until cheese begins to brown and biscuits are firm.

JOHN'S BAKED APPLE CRUMBLE AND ORGANIC SWEET CREAM

The Baxters love keeping dessert simple. Fruit is very sweet, and when cooked it's even sweeter. Add a few ingredients and real, organic homemade whipped cream and you have a dessert better than anything store-bought. Once when John was going through a box of his parents' things, he came across this recipe. He modified it and now John's Baked Apple Crumble is not only simple to make but the family's favorite dessert. Simply follow these directions:

* Preheat oven to 350 degrees.
* Core and peel 14 medium apples.
* Slice the apples and place in a 13-by-9-inch baking dish.
* Sprinkle 2 teaspoons of cinnamon over the apples.
* Pour 1/4 cup of melted butter over the apples.
* Sprinkle with 1/4 cup of Swerve confectioners' sugar.
* In a separate bowl mix 1 cup almond flour, 1/4 cup Swerve and 1 stick melted butter. Mix well, then sprinkle over the apple mixture.
* Stir well and bake for 2 hours at 350 degrees.
* In a separate bowl, pour 1-2 pints of organic heavy cream. Add 1 teaspoon of vanilla for each pint. Add 2 tablespoons of Swerve confectioners' sugar per pint. Beat until soft peaks form.

✻ Serve hot, topped with the fresh whipped cream. Enjoy.

ONE CHANCE FOUNDATION

The Kingsbury Family is passionate about seeing orphans all over the world brought home to their forever families. As a result, they created the One Chance Foundation!

This foundation was inspired by the memory of Karen's father, Ted C. Kingsbury. Ted always said, "Life is not a dress rehearsal. We have one chance to love, one chance to truly live!" Karen often tells her reader friends that they have "one chance to write the story of their lives!"

Now with Karen's One Chance Foundation, readers can join her in the belief that all of us have one chance to make a difference in the lives of orphans.

In the Bible, James 1:27 says that true Christians ought to care for orphans. The One Chance Foundation was created with that truth in mind.

If you are interested in giving to Karen's One Chance Foundation and having your

dedication printed in one of Karen's up-
coming novels, visit www.KarenKingsbury
.com and click on the Foundation tab.

The following dedications were made by
some of Karen's readers, who forever are
making a difference in the lives of orphans
around the world.

* With Love & Appreciation to Karen &
  David Bressel — The One Chance
  Foundation
* Betty O'Neil — you have shown much
  courage & strength in your struggle with
  cancer for so many years. Your friendship has given me inspiration, joy, &
  love. God has blessed me by including
  you in my life! — Brenda Lacey
* To Mom; Thank you for choosing to be
  my mom. Love, Your Angel, Jen
* Rachel, Court & Alex — I am so blessed
  to be your Mom! — Mera
* To Mom, Lili Kukkola for her Finnish
  SISU & trusting in God. Love, Jan
* I thank God for the blessing of my
  husband, Dave Miller. Love, Jan
* To Kathy Conquest, my heart-to-heart
  prayer warrior! — Jan
* To Nancy Bayne, ever ready for a bon-
  bon chat! — Jan
* With Love & Appreciation to Jan Kuk-

kola — The One Chance Foundation

❉ Sean, Patrick & Michael — We'll love you forever! Mom & Dad

❉ I love you Kira, Austin, Peyton, and Johnny — Mom

❉ With love, Mary Sgro

❉ To orphans everywhere, with love, Jan

❉ Forever and always loved. For Harper

❉ To God who provides and created me to be the person I am! — Jamie Smith

❉ Susan Kane, you're the BEST in all you do! Thank you! — Love, Team KK

❉ With love, Deborah Rogers

❉ Sweet Madelyne, Your love & joy light up my life! Love, Mommy

❉ Dedicated to my loving wife & nights falling asleep listening to stories by Karen on her Kindle. — Love, Jay Hall

❉ My dear friend, Karen Baker. Thanks for introducing me to Karen Kingsbury Books. Much love, Doris

❉ JoAnn, you are very special to me! Love, Jessica

❉ To the love of my life, John. Through thick & thin, 33 years & counting. Love you so much — Kathy

❉ In memory of Caryl Shearer — who shared her love and her books! — Kim

❉ In loving memory of Amy Carnagey — Love, Luke

* With love & appreciation to the Carnagey Family! — The One Chance Foundation
* With love, Abby Oberlin
* Kylie + Caroline: Chase God, dream big, and love hard. — Mama
* To My Mom, Sherry. Please feel better soon! Love U! ~Andrea
* Blessings to Dan & Emily on their wedding day. — Love, Becky Carroll
* Mom, when I pick up a book, I think of you. Love, Melinda
* Blessings to my dear grandmother, Josephine! — In Faith & Love, Cheryl
* "Matthew" One woman's sacrifice became a gift from God to our family! — Debbie
* We love and miss you Mom/Grandma — Love, Sandy, Sarah & Mariah
* Merry Christmas Zach, Katie & Luke Hamilton. Love, Mom/Mimi
* Love our great kids, Steve, Mike & Patty, & 7 gr-kids! Mom E
* To God — for blessings of life, love, & laughter! K&S Holman
* For our courageous Aubrey G, from your cruise buddies
* Happy 77th Donna, our favorite KK fan! Love, the Carter Kids
* Shirley Collins, I admire your dedica-

tion to the Lord! — Becky Day

❋ Amber Nicole Holberg, Keep reading Karen Kingsbury novels! — Nana B

❋ To the Waitresses, Chefs & Owner at The Court Cafe & Pub, Louisa, VA — Becky Day

❋ With love, Robyn Stiles

❋ Diana Dittus — you have a true heart of gold. Love, Your Family

❋ Mom, who blesses us all with her love & kindness. Love, Tika

❋ In honor of our mother, Violet Studer. Love from the kids!

❋ To Karen, For always listening to Him! Jeremiah 29:11 — We love you!

ABOUT THE AUTHOR

Karen Kingsbury, #1 *New York Times* bestselling novelist, is America's favorite inspirational storyteller, with more than twenty-five million copies of her award-winning books in print. Her last dozen titles have topped bestseller lists and many of her novels are under development with Hallmark Films and as major motion pictures. She lives in Tennessee with her husband, Don, and their five sons, three of whom are adopted from Haiti. Their actress daughter, Kelsey, lives nearby and is married to Christian recording artist Kyle Kupecky. The couple recently welcomed their first child, Hudson.